D1175681

Beware the Guns of Iron Eyes

Iron Eyes finds himself staring at a forest. A forest that reminds him of a time long before he had become the scarred infamous bounty hunter he now was.

As he waits for his beloved Squirrel Sally to show up on her stagecoach, his mind drifts back to how it had all started.

Iron Eyes remembers the time when he first set foot out of the forest where he had grown to manhood. The forest was where he had been abandoned as a baby and raised by timber wolves.

Beware the Guns of Iron Eyes

Rory Black

A Black Horse Western

ROBERT HALE

© Rory Black 2018
First published in Great Britain 2018

ISBN 978-0-7198-2753-2

The Crowood Press
The Stable Block
Crowood Lane
Ramsbury
Marlborough
Wiltshire SN8 2HR

www.bhwesterns.com

Robert Hale is an imprint
of The Crowood Press

Typeset by
Derek Doyle & Associates, Shaw Heath
Printed and bound in Great Britain by
4edge Limited

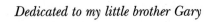

Dedicated to my little brother Gary

PROLOGUE

Few who had ever set eyes upon the hideously maimed creature, known throughout the Wild West as Iron Eyes the bounty hunter, could ever have imagined the horrors that he had endured since he had first opened his eyes and filled his lungs with precious air. Iron Eyes would grow to adulthood in the eerie twilight of a vast forest filled with deadly animals and venomous serpents. Abandoned at birth by an unknown mother due some misplaced notion of shame, the newly born baby would survive only because of a pack of timber wolves' instinctive kindness. The wolves would raise and teach him the ways of the wild. It was a debt for which he would be eternally thankful.

Iron Eyes was one of those rare creatures, a feral child. More animal than human in his ways, this gave him the swiftness to outwit all that tried to end his short existence once and for all.

Many have wondered about the hideously scarred

bounty hunter and how his unique story had started. Had they known how he had become the almost mythical and infamous bounty hunter who roamed the West with his smoking Navy Colts gripped in his skeletal hands, they might have understood the tall emaciated figure a little better.

Even the most fertile of imaginations, however, could never have envisioned that anything that looked the way he did could ever have once appeared normal.

But he had.

Long before he was covered in the scars of his seemingly endless battles, Iron Eyes had been an enigmatic figure. It was said that the Indians who roamed the vast forest knew who and what Iron Eyes truly was, but even they did not know the whole truth.

It was rumoured that they also knew where he had come from, but they remained silent. In reality the Indians were no wiser to the origins of the infamous Iron Eyes than anyone else, but they would embellish his myth around their campfires. Every telling would add just a little bit more to the man they had grown to think of as a ghost.

During his childhood, the wolves had taught Iron Eyes to remain out of his enemies' line of sight. The Indians' campfire stories interpreted this as meaning that he was not actually a living man like themselves. The reason they had never been able to stop him stealing their weaponry or their fresh kills was because Iron Eyes was already dead.

Even the greatest Indian bowman could not be expected to kill a phantom. As a young boy who had moved unseen and unheard through the dense undergrowth to taunt the Indians, Iron Eyes had became a thorn in their collective sides. In the mythology that grew around Iron Eyes, he became known by the title Ayan-Ees, the evil spirit.

For years until he reached maturity, Iron Eyes had honed the ways of the wolf and stolen anything he needed or simply desired from their traps and encampments.

Resentment had grown into hatred.

Iron Eyes disliked them as much as they hated him.

Year by year the Indian tales became taller with each telling. Secreted above the Indians' camps with only tree canopies to hide him from view, Iron Eyes had listened to the Indians so often that he actually understood their language.

Just like the stories that still prevail in the wilderness across the vast land, the Indians would find his footprints along the muddy trails. Yet no matter how hard they tried, they could never actually see him clearly. In time the footprints grew larger, just as Iron Eyes himself developed into a tall agile young man.

Iron Eyes would climb the tallest trees and stare out from the forest at the glowing amber lights of a nearby logging town. Silver Creek's coal oil lanterns glowed in the darkness and intrigued the inquisitive youngster. He was curious as to what sort of people dwelled in the unfamiliar houses he could just make out from his perilous perch.

This was when Iron Eyes realized that there was another world beyond the limits of the woodlands he roamed. A place where he might not have to dodge the arrows of those who tried to kill him as they had also done to most of the timber wolves that had raised him.

Could the glowing settlement be the safe haven he had always craved? The thought grew like a cancer in his curious mind for months. Life in the forest had grown tedious for the young hunter and he grew weary of forever remaining in the shadows so that he could avoid the Indians' arrows.

He had spotted several of the lumberjacks who were gradually clearing the hills and noticed that they covered their bodies in clothing like the Indians did during the winter months.

Iron Eyes was intelligent enough to realize that if he were to venture into the town, he would have to fashion some sort of clothing for himself. Using leather from his animal pelts and anything else he could lay his hands upon, he somehow managed to make a crude shirt and pants that he thought resembled what he had seen the lumberjacks wearing.

Somehow Iron Eyes even managed to cobble together a pair of boots. Before setting out for the town, Iron Eyes decided to test out his crude appearance on his mortal enemies and let them catch sight

10

of him. For the first time in his life the gaunt hunter no longer hid from view amid the numerous shadows of the forest. The sudden sight of the tall emaciated youngster terrified most of the Indians as they had never seen him clearly before.

Now it was their turn to run and hide. The creature they had built up so many stories about was suddenly real to them and appeared even more lethal-looking than any of their tall-tales.

This reaction gave Iron Eyes even more confidence than he already had. It was his height that troubled the Indians the most, for he was at least a foot taller than any of the forest warriors.

His tall lean frame and mane of long jet black hair gave him the appearance of a noble prince belonging to some strange forgotten tribe.

Perhaps that was what he actually was.

Nobody would ever know for sure.

His appearance was not actually like that of any of the native braves that he constantly encountered, though. Neither did he resemble any of the white settlers who slowly but surely made their way across the once sacred land where he had grown up.

Iron Eyes was an enigma. He simply did not fit in either camp. The Indians had grown to hate him due to his uncanny hunting skills, and the whites he would eventually encounter considered him to be something akin to an Apache spy. It had not taken the fearless misfit long to realize that he did not belong to either of the opposing sides.

11

He would soon discover that most men feared him for some unknown reason. Unfortunately men always try to destroy or kill such things.

Curiosity lured the hunter out from the dense forested mountains and begin his long trek into lands which he neither understood or cared for. Soon, however, he would bury his misgivings beneath a waterfall of firewater and cheap cigars.

Unlike his despised enemies, the whiskey he either traded or stole had no effect on his pitifully lean body or deadly keen mind. Somehow he could drink as much of the fiery liquid as he desired with no ill effects.

Although Iron Eyes would never fit into the land where most of us dwell, he simply could not prevent himself from continuing on his long blood-stained journey. Once the naïve youngster left the relative safety of the forest, he found his curiosity impossible to resist. No matter how much pain he suffered in civilization, he simply could not stop moving forward.

Most men, it is said, are buried less than a stone's throw away from where they were born. They never dare leave the place where they feel safe. Some like Iron Eyes seek the one thing they may never find and are willing to suffer the brutal atrocities fate throws at them during their often futile quest.

This is the story of Iron Eyes before he became hideously mutilated by the bullets, arrows and knives of his countless foes. An almost forgotten time when the gaunt creature crawled out from the safety of the forest and discovered that his hunting skills were better suited to hunting down and killing wanted men for bounty money.

This is the beginning.

But beware the guns.

Beware the guns of Iron Eyes.

ONE

The sight of the lone horseman was enough to stop the numerous birds from singing and freeze the hearts of anyone that might have cast their innocent attention in his direction. The skeletal figure who sat astride his magnificent palomino stallion appeared to have come from the bowels of Hell itself. He sat motionless on his high-shouldered mount and studied the forest before him and began to remember things he had thought were long forgotten.

A stiff breeze raced across the barren hillside like a freight train and moved the tall grass between his mount and the dark untamed forest. His mutilated face watched the strangely familiar sight as thoughts drifted from hunting down another wanted outlaw to memories of a time when things were less dramatic.

His long bony fingers touched his face and traced

14

across the disfigured flesh that covered his skull, reminding him of a time when there were no hideous reminders of his many injuries.

Iron Eyes bore the scars of countless fights. Every battle he had waged during his lifetime showed on his mutilated face. Draped in an oversized trail coat and hunched over his ornate saddle, his mind drifted back to when he too resembled regular folk.

His hands began to search his many pockets for a cigar in a vain effort to chase the thoughts from his mind. The infamous bounty hunter believed that tobacco smoke was a cure for all ills. As the long-legged horseman sat astride the powerful palomino and wondered why his thoughts were tormenting him, he started to remember things he had considered dead and buried. Long before he had left the forest that had been his home to seek something he still had not found, Iron Eyes had lived a secluded existence. Yet even back then he had craved something more.

Iron Eyes pulled a long thin cigar from his inside pocket and placed it between his teeth. His thumbnail scratched a match and raised the fiery stick to the end of the twisted tobacco stick. He puffed so that a cloud of smoke hung around his wide shoulders until it was caught by the breeze and vanished across the rolling hills.

Iron Eyes glanced over his shoulder. The trail that his large horse had made in the high grass was evident and he wondered how long it would be

15

before Squirrel Sally drove her stagecoach after him and created an even wider scar on the hillside. The notorious bounty hunter returned his narrowed eyes to the forest ahead of him. He filled his lungs with acrid smoke and savoured its flavour for a few moments before exhaling. This time the cigar smoke did not stop the memories from sweeping over Iron Eyes as he rested himself and his exhausted mount.

His razor sharp teeth gripped the cigar as his cruelly scarred eyes stared at the forest. Memories flooded back. This land resembled his birthplace and yet was over a hundred miles from where he had first set out on his unfulfilled quest.

Few, if any knew of his true origins.

Until this very moment even Iron Eyes had forgotten how his life had changed so drastically and brought him to where he now found himself. As smoke burned his unblinking eyes, the decrepit horseman rested his bony wrists on the silver saddle horn and allowed the long-repressed memories to return.

His usually emotionless heart began to pound inside his chest like an Apache war drum. Iron Eyes had never allowed himself to remember many of the events from long ago and yet now seemed unable to stop them from engulfing him.

He started to recall the time before he had sold his soul to the Devil to become a bounty hunter. Iron Eyes lowered his head and began to remember when the only thing he ever hunted was animals to fill his belly.

That had been before unbridled curiosity had drawn him out into the world of the white man. A time when a scrawny young misfit had taken a gigantic step from one world into another.

Iron Eyes reached back to his saddlebags, lifted the flap of one of its satchels and pulled out one of his many whiskey bottles. He pulled its cork. The familiar aroma of the hard liquor only added more fuel to the memories which were stampeding back into his mind.

He closed his eyes and took a long swig.

The tall young man wandered out of the forest and stared up at the vast cloudless blue sky. This was the first time that he had ever seen the heavens without having to look up through the tree canopies before. Each of the other occasions that he had left the forest had been after sundown. Now the gaunt figure was venturing to the nearby town during the hours of daylight. Iron Eyes had gotten to know several of the town's inhabitants since he had first braved the strange new world which some laughingly called civilization. Now as the noon high sun beat down upon the small settlement the unusual looking young man felt confident to let others cast their eyes upon him.

Apart from the seductive taste of cigars and the gut burning rotgut whiskey, the town offered nothing

17

which he cared for. Yet something deep in his craw told him that this new world was where he ought to be because this was where he would find his destiny. Iron Eyes was unsure whether he cared for it or not but was driven by insatiable curiosity.

Iron Eyes brushed the sweat off his brow and narrowed his eyes against the merciless light which seemed to reflect off the very ground itself. He had no experience of such brightness and did not fully understand it. If it were not for the lure of the cigars and whiskey, Iron Eyes might have turned and headed back into the depths of the forest.

At least it was cool there, he thought.

The long-haired youth cut a strange looking figure as his spindly legs cut a path through the tall grass toward the wagon trail road which was used by the loggers that were gradually reducing the forest to a mere fraction of its original size.

His hand-crafted clothes fitted but bore little resemblance to anything worn by his contemporaries. Yet those in the town that had encountered Iron Eyes on his previous visits had not dared mention this for fear of enraging the odd looking character.

It was quite obvious to all who had set eyes upon him that Iron Eyes was what was commonly known as a wild man. A feral creature that was more animal than man.

As Iron Eyes clambered up on to the trail road he sighed and stared ahead at his destination through the shimmering haze that shimmered before his screwed-up eyes. The blisteringly hot sun was burning his flesh like acid and his hands felt as though a thousand hornets had attacked his skin.

Iron Eyes had never known such a painful sensation before and did not like it, but the thought of the whiskey and the flavoursome cigars kept him walking.

The thought that his unusual appearance might draw some to mock him simply did not cross his mind. He knew nothing of the ways of his fellow men apart from the various Indian warriors who had tried to kill him his entire life.

Soon Iron Eyes would discover that some men somehow do not have the brains they were born with. They tend to turn on those that they deem different to themselves and that could be a mighty dangerous thing to do in the Wild West.

For sometimes even the smallest of dogs have sharp teeth.

The tall figure carried a long knife in the neck of his right boot and had a bow over his shoulder with a quiver of arrows attached to his belt. Iron Eyes might have appeared odd to most who spied him as he approached the outskirts of the town, but he was nevertheless formidable.

Killing meant nothing to Iron Eyes, but until now he had restricted his lethal hunting skills to animals and any Indians that attacked him. Survival meant you either killed or ended up dead yourself.

There was no alternative.

19

In the world where he was heading, just like the one behind his wide shoulders, there were unwritten rules which nobody was allowed to forsake.

Soon Iron Eyes would discover this deadly fact.

TWO

The heat mercilessly continued to burn down upon the rough ground between the settlement and the tree-covered hills. Iron Eyes ran his long bony fingers through his sweat-soaked hair and then snarled like a wild beast at the savage sun which relentlessly tormented his flesh.

Just like the timber wolves that had raised him, Iron Eyes was not used to the feeling of unrelenting heat. It might have sapped his strength if not for the thought that kept him heading straight toward Silver Creek.

Iron Eyes could almost taste the whiskey he craved as well as the powerful cigars. Just the thought of those two items kept his boots moving along the trail road.

He stared across the rolling hills to the small settlement he could see through the rising heat haze, as beads of sweat dripped from the strands of hair which hung over his face. His imaginative mind considered the people he would discover in the small town on this visit. The notion appealed to him.

Daylight would bring far more folks on to its streets, he told himself.

His previous visits had been uneventful and the high-shouldered youth imagined wrongly that this time would be the same. Iron Eyes had only bumped into a few of the town's menfolk as he traded his furs and bought whiskey and smokes. Most of its citizens had been safely tucked into their beds on those occasions.

This time he dared to visit during daylight.

Naïvely he continued walking.

Iron Eyes had ventured from the forest only a handful of times before to trade animal furs to Kermit Lang, the proprietor of the hardware store, for whiskey and cigars. The forest did not have anything like the taste of either and each time he visited, he wanted more.

At first Iron Eyes had not understood what the people were saying but he was a quick learner and soon picked up enough of their words to get by, thanks to help of the stout blacksmith Bo Hartson. Hartson had taken an interest in the young hunter and shared his interest in whiskey.

Iron Eyes did not realize it, but he had an uncanny ability to decipher most spoken languages and become fluent in them very quickly.

The blacksmith was curious about his young pupil

and coached Iron Eyes every time he visited the livery. Hartson knew that he would learn more about the unusual Iron Eyes the more he taught him to speak English. Just like the younger man, he was a curious character.

As his long thin legs drew him closer to the town, Iron Eyes looked down at the three furs dangling from his belt and nodded to himself.

They would bring him enough whiskey and cigars to keep him happy for a while, he thought. As he got even closer he noticed something happening within the unmarked boundaries of the settlement.

His curiosity was wetted.

What was going on? His curious mind wondered.

The commotion reminded Iron Eyes of the warriors back in the forest when he had outwitted them and stolen their latest kill. Yet this was no bunch of warriors ranting angrily, this was excited white men cheering about something that Iron Eyes did not understand.

He increased his pace.

THREE

The naïve Iron Eyes had never witnessed anything quite like it before and was drawn like a moth to a naked flame into Silver Creek. His calculating eyes darted around the strangely busy thoroughfare to ensure that this was not a trap to capture his hide. Not one of the inhabitants of the remote settlement was looking at the young hunter, though. They all seemed to be gathered at the far end of the long street. There was something far more interesting there. At least they thought it was far more interesting.

Iron Eyes continued walking into Silver Creek. With each step he tightened his eyes in a bid to see whatever it was that was causing all the excitement.

Then he saw it.

But what he saw made no sense to him. He still could not comprehend what it was he was actually witnessing. A roped off section of the main street was the focus of their cheering and booing. Two very

24

large lumberjacks were stripped to the waist and slugging it out for all they were worth. With each blow the crowd clapped and cheered.

Blood covered both of the men as they pounded at one another with bare fists. Iron Eyes had seen stags rutting and bears ripping one another to shreds, but he had never seen grown men getting physically violent for no apparent reason before.

Two well-built examples of logging men were battling it out as a group of others gathered around the ropes. By the size of the crowd, the tall hunter imagined that nearly all of the town's inhabitants were surrounding the roped-off area watching the fight.

Some were cheering and others were just screaming in anger as they waved handfuls of bank notes at the two bruised and bloodied battlers.

Was this some ritual? The young hunter wondered. Why would anyone risk being crippled – or worse – in this way? So many questions flashed through his mind, yet not one logical answer presented itself.

Iron Eyes stepped up on to a sidewalk beside the tall livery stable, ambled along its length and rested a shoulder against one of its open barn doors. The fight continued and grew no less bloody.

He was mesmerised by the spectacle, even though he had no idea what was happening. Not a single member of the townsfolk noticed the stranger with the mane of long black hair who was observing the brutal contest. Droplets of blood flew skyward as a flurry of punches from one of the fighters found its target.

It was as if the entire population of Silver Creek was in the street watching the fight. Buckets of water were thrown over the two exhausted fighters to revive them and then the battle continued.

Iron Eyes rubbed his bony fingers along his jawline. He had seen the Indians of the forest doing many strange things during his life but nothing like this. This was beyond his ability to make sense of.

Was this one of the white men's customs?

Before he had time to absorb the thought, he heard something behind him moving from the dark interior of the livery toward his wide back. He was not alarmed for he had heard the footsteps before on his previous visits. The sound of heavy boots behind the youngster drew Iron Eyes' attention. He glanced over his shoulder at the sweat-soaked figure of Bo Hartson as he moved out into the sunlight.

Iron Eyes gave a sharp nod of his head in silent greeting.

'Howdy, Iron Eyes,' the burly blacksmith grunted with amusement as he sucked on the stem of his spent pipe and nodded back at Iron Eyes. Bo Hartson rested his hairy shoulders against the barn door and then struck a match and cupped its flame above the pipe bowl. 'Reckon I spooked you, huh?'

'Spooked me?' Iron Eyes repeated the unfamiliar words as he returned the gleaming knife back into its leather sheath.

'I scared you,' Hartson added and tossed his match at the sand. 'I spooked you.'

Iron Eyes nodded.

'You spooked me, Bo,' he agreed.

'What you doing in Silver Creek?' the blacksmith asked through a cloud of pipe smoke. 'Don't tell me you run out of whiskey already.'

The young misfit nodded.

'And cigars all gone,' Iron Eyes sighed as he turned his head and peered through the long strands on his hair at the street fight fifty yards from where he was standing. 'I come to trade.'

Hartson smiled as his teeth gripped the pipe stem.

'This has gotta be the first time you showed up here in the daytime, ain't it?' he noted as he silently studied the pitifully lean youngster that he felt sorry for. 'You usually come here after sundown.'

Iron Eyes nodded and then pointed at the fight.

'What is this?' he wondered as the two men started to use more than just their fists. 'Why do men fight like that and why are all the other folks shouting? This is very strange and I do not understand.'

The blacksmith rested his hands on his hips thoughtfully.

'Ain't you ever seen a prize fight before, boy?' Hartson asked his young companion. 'Them loggers are fighting to make money.'

'Why?' Iron Eyes frowned as he watched the crowd getting even more animated the longer the fight progressed.

27

'Money, Iron Eyes,' the blacksmith attempted to explain. 'Them numbskulls are fighting for money. The winner will get fifty bucks.'

'They get dollars to do that?' Iron Eyes could not hide his surprise. He ran his bony fingers through his lengthy hair and dragged it off his face. 'That don't make any sense, Bo. Do they have to kill to get dollars?'

The blacksmith roared with laughter and patted his hips with his massive hands. He turned his lean friend until they were staring into one another's eyes.

'Nope, they don't have to kill,' Hartson answered and then had a second thought. 'But it does happen every now and then in some of the prize fights. The last big fight lasted eighty-three rounds and one of the idiots died. Them boys are so proud they just ain't got the brains to get themselves knocked out.'

'Eighty-three rounds,' Iron Eyes repeated and then looked away from the blacksmith. 'Is that a long time?'

'A mighty long time, boy,' Hartson tapped Iron Eyes' shoulder to draw his attention. 'Are you thirsty? I mean real thirsty for something a damn sight stronger than water. Are you?'

The youngster grinned and nodded.

'Yep,' the young hunter replied.

The larger man winked and jerked his head. 'Come and help me polish off a bottle of rye. There ain't no business to be had when they got the street roped off.'

'What is rye?' Iron Eyes asked innocently. 'Is it whiskey?'

'It sure is, boy,' Hartson turned and headed back into the shade of the livery stable. 'Best whiskey in Silver Creek. Come and help me empty the bottle.'

Iron Eyes hesitated and gripped the furs hanging from his belt.

'But I have to trade furs for dollars,' he said.

The muscular Hartson sat down next to his forge and gestured at the young hunter to join him. He patted an upturned barrel with his large hand.

'All the stores are locked up until the fight ends,' he informed his friend. 'You ain't gonna sell them furs for hours yet, so get your bony ass over here and sit down. We got some supping to do.'

Iron Eyes nodded, then walked to the forge and sat down on the upturned barrel next to his jovial pal. He watched as Hartson reached into a dark space beneath the glowing coals of the forge and pulled out a full bottle of whiskey and showed it to his companion.

'Ain't that a pretty sight, Iron Eyes?' the large man said before pulling its cork from the bottle neck with his teeth and spitting it on to the coals.

'Very pretty,' the hunter agreed as he caught the scent of the powerful liquor in his flared nostrils. 'Smells good.'

Hartson aimed a large finger at a shelf where two tin cups rested amid soot and dust. 'Get them mugs, boy. We got us some serious drinking to do.'

Iron Eyes did not need to be told twice. He quickly got to his feet and grabbed the tin cups and shook the dust from them. He held them and watched as the liveryman filled both tin vessels with the amber liquor. The fumes filled both their nostrils.

'Smells good,' Iron Eyes drooled.

'It sure does,' Hartson took one of the cups and nodded to the young man to sit back down next to him. 'Drink up, sonny. We got us a lot of dust to wash down our throats.'

Iron Eyes lifted the cup to his lips and took a big swallow. The fiery liquor burned a trail down into his gullet and caused Iron Eyes to sigh heavily as the fumes filled his head.

'Good whiskey,' he smiled.

The blacksmith lifted his cup and took a swallow himself of the amber nectar. As its fumes rose up from his ample belly, a satisfied smile traced Hartson's face.

'Damn,' he agreed. 'That is good rye. I bet this brew ain't rotgut. This stuff tastes genuine.'

Iron Eyes did not understand anything the man in the long leather apron was saying, but nodded in agreement anyway. He took another gulp of the liquor in his cup and gave out a huge sigh.

Bo Hartson finished his ration and then refilled both the tin cups. He watched as the youngster eagerly drank the powerful liquor and thought how he had first encountered the strange youngster one dark night only weeks before.

He had been just finishing tending to the horses in the livery when he caught sight of the youngster looking like a frightened mountain cat caught in torchlight. At first Iron Eyes had done what all scared creatures do and moved into the shadows as if to hide, yet the youngster's curiosity had soon overwhelmed his caution.

Hartson had been surprised by the sight of the tall figure, who eventually summoned enough courage to enter the vast interior of the livery. The blacksmith knew immediately that there was something unusual about Iron Eyes.

For one thing, Iron Eyes could not speak any known language that Hartson understood. The words the youngster uttered sounded a lot like one of the thousands of Indian dialects. Yet it was obvious that although Iron Eyes had heard others speak, he himself had never spoken.

The big man had felt sorry for the youngster.

Iron Eyes found it easier to make noises. He simply grunted and pointed at anything and everything that caught his interest. The large livery stable owner had patiently managed to teach the gaunt, emaciated youngster a few words so that they could communicate.

With each occasional visit, Hartson had taught him more and more words. Iron Eyes seemed to have only two interests in what the blacksmith laughingly called civilization.

Whiskey and cigars.

There seemed to be nothing else that Iron Eyes desired in Silver Creek. Hartson was taken by the way the youngster, compared to others of his age, did not appear to want the things most youngsters wanted. There was not an envious bone in his young body. As long as he could get hold of cigars and hard liquor, he was satisfied.

Luckily for his mentor, Iron Eyes had been a fast learner and had an incredible memory. When Hartson had asked what his name was he blurted out something which Hartson imagined was what the Indians in the forests must have called him.

'Indians call me Ayan-Ees,' Iron Eyes had said and then added. 'I think it mean the evil one.'

The blacksmith had interpreted the name as Iron Eyes and from that moment on, that was what the youngster would answer when asked his name. The name would remain with him for the rest of his life.

Hartson refilled their tin cups again. He was amazed how quickly his young pupil grasped English and how his use of the language improved with every meeting.

Iron Eyes sipped his whiskey while Hartson looked at him with curiosity. The blacksmith had a thousand questions for the youngster but knew that he would have to wait until Iron Eyes was capable of answering.

As Hartson sipped his whiskey, he realized that Iron Eyes appeared to have never encountered people before, yet that seemed impossible to the blacksmith. How could anyone grow to well over six feet in height without ever having met other folks?

Yet that was the only conclusion Hartson could come to as they drank beside the warm forge. It was as if Iron Eyes had come from another world where there were no folks like the large blacksmith and his fellow townsfolk.

Iron Eyes had mentioned Indians, but he had said that they hunted him the way he hunted animals. They feared him for some unknown reason, which the blacksmith could only guess at.

Hartson concluded that everything he took as being normal was utterly alien to Iron Eyes. He was like a surprised animal with every new object he encountered. Hartson simply could not fathom who or what his drinking companion actually was. He wondered how on earth Iron Eyes could have possibly grown to manhood alone in the forest.

He knew that most of the townsfolk would not survive a week in there, but this young man seemed to have beaten the odds and done exactly that.

Hartson leaned forward and poured more whiskey into Iron Eyes' cup. Then he recalled the various tribes of Indians which had once plagued Silver Creek for several years. He wondered if they were still in the forest and, if so, how had Iron Eyes managed to avoid them for so long.

'Tell me something, boy,' the large man started.

The bullet-coloured eyes, which he would one day become famous for, darted at the blacksmith. Iron Eyes watched and listened to the first person he had ever met who had never attempted to harm him.

Hartson did not know it, but Iron Eyes considered his drinking companion to be his only friend.

Having managed to get the youngster's full attention, Hartson pressed on with his questioning and hoped that Iron Eyes' limited knowledge of his new language would be able to understand him.

'Have you always lived in them woods, boy?' he began.

Iron Eyes nodded as he lifted the cup to his lips and took a mouthful of whiskey. His eyes were fixed on the blacksmith as the burly man continued.

'Tell me something,' Hartson started. 'Are you an Injun?'

Suddenly Iron Eyes expression changed. It was as though he had been insulted or physically hurt and took the blacksmith by surprise.

There was a fire in the eyes of the young hunter. Iron Eyes looked far angrier than the older man had anticipated and started to make a chilling noise. It was a guttural growl like a ravenous timber wolf. Hartson leaned back on his makeshift seat and started to tremble with fear as the growl grew louder.

Hartson felt his heart quicken as Iron Eyes glared at him with unblinking eyes. They burned through the blacksmith as the young hunter continued to growl as though he were about to leap straight at him. Drool dripped from his razor sharp teeth and Iron Eyes began to pant like a rabid wolf.

The blacksmith had never been so terrified. This

was the first time that he had seen his young friend completely change from a quiet youngster into something that he felt was more akin to a wild animal.

'You OK, Iron Eyes?' he stammered fearfully.

There was no reply. Just the continuing panting and low guttural growling that sent shivers rippling through his seated body. Desperately Hartson tried to think of what he had said that might have caused Iron Eyes to become so angry. Yet no matter how hard he tried, all he could think of was what the youngster might do next.

'Easy, Iron Eyes,' he blurted. 'I didn't mean to hurt you.'

Iron Eyes lowered his head until his face was hidden by his mane of long thick hair. The whiskey started to splash from the tin cup in Hartson's large hand. He wanted to turn and run but he knew that was impossible. The blacksmith realized that he would never even get to his feet before the furious youngster leapt from where he sat.

'Take it easy, boy. I didn't mean to rile you up,' Hartson said as he felt his heart pounding frantically inside his chest. It felt as though it might burst at any moment.

The words seemed to fall on deaf ears as Iron Eyes crouched on the barrel and stared through his limp black locks at the blacksmith.

Then as the growling grew louder and louder, Iron Eyes pulled his bow off his shoulder and charged its taut string with an arrow.

'What you gonna do, Iron Eyes?' Hartson yelped like a wounded hound as he stared at the drawstring being pulled back by the bony hands until the flint arrowhead was touching the wooden bow shaft.

FOUR

At unimaginable speed, Iron Eyes swung on his heels, released the arrow and then before the bow string had stopped vibrating, placed another arrow in its place. The slender projectile hummed like a crazed hornet as it cut through the livery stable and vanished into the shadows of an empty stall. The muscular blacksmith gasped as he heard the unmistakable sound of a rat squeal in the darkest part of the massive structure.

Iron Eyes stood like a gaunt statue until his temper had eased and the unfortunate rodent had succumbed to death. The hunter then snorted and relaxed the bowstring before returning the fresh arrow back into its quiver. Without uttering a word, he returned the bow to his shoulder and sat down again. He picked up his tin mug and downed the remainder of its fiery contents.

The youngster exhaled and looked back into

Hartson's still fearful face. He was silent, but breathing heavily as he held the tin mug in his bony hands.

'You OK, boy?' Hartson fearfully asked.

Iron Eyes nodded and then warned.

'Never call me an Injun, Bo,' he quietly whispered. 'I don't like Injuns.'

'How come?' the blacksmith hastily refilled both their tin cups as he felt his heart start to resume its less rapid pounding.

'I don't like anyone who don't like me,' Iron Eyes replied coldly.

Hartson took a gulp of whiskey, 'What you mean?'

The young hunter looked at his reflection in the whiskey in his cup. The blacksmith had never seen his friend so serious before. Finally Iron Eyes inhaled deeply and answered.

'They try to kill Iron Eyes,' the younger man said after taking a gulp of his whiskey. 'They have always try to kill me. They no like me, so I do not like them.'

'Sounds reasonable,' Hartson agreed before taking a big swallow of the amber liquor and allowing its fumes to bathe him in an ample ration of Dutch courage.

Iron Eyes rubbed his face with the bony digits of his left hand and sighed heavily. 'Ever since I can recall, the Injuns have hunted me. They treat me as if I were a critter.'

'How come they don't like you?' the blacksmith asked.

Iron Eyes shook his head. 'I do not know. They

talk about me around their campfires and say that I am a Devil. I must be destroyed before I destroy them. I do not savvy.'

Bo Hartson rubbed the sweat off his whiskers thoughtfully and leaned closer to his friend.

'It sounds to me like they fear you, Iron Eyes,' he said wisely before adding. 'Folks tend to try and kill things that scare them. Like swatting flies or crushing spiders underfoot. They just do it.'

'Why?' Iron Eyes wondered.

'If we knew the answer to that we'd be a whole lot smarter than we are, sonny,' the larger man grinned. 'It's the way folks are, no matter what colour they are.'

Iron Eyes narrowed his eyes and looked straight at the big man sat three feet from where he rested his own much younger bones.

'You think I look like an Injun?' he asked.

Hartson felt uncomfortable with the question and took another swallow of the fiery whiskey before answering.

'Not really,' he carefully ventured. 'It's just you got long black hair like most of the Injuns I've ever set eyes upon. Apart from that you don't actually look like one of them at all.'

'Why not?'

'You're way too tall for one thing,' Hartson said.

Iron Eyes frowned. 'So I look like a white man?'

The blacksmith rubbed his neck. 'Hell, you don't actually look like any white man that I've ever set eyes

39

upon, boy. You don't act like one either.'

Iron Eyes finished his whiskey and held out his cup again as he tried to work out what the blacksmith had meant. His lack of understanding angered the pitifully thin youngster.

'So I do not look like a white man and I do not look like Injun?' he muttered as he watched his cup being filled. 'What do I look like then?'

Bo Hartson poured the last of the liquor into his cup and tossed the empty bottle across the livery. He cleared his throat carefully and looked at his companion in a fatherly way.

'I reckon you're unique, Iron Eyes,' he said tactfully. 'A one of a kind sort of critter. There ain't nobody like you, boy. You should be proud of that.'

Iron Eyes leaned back on the upturned barrel and looked at the liveryman through strands of his limp hair. 'I no savvy.'

'Me neither, sonny,' Hartson chuckled. 'I ain't sure that anyone could ever figure you out.'

'Is that good?'

Hartson nodded and slapped the hunter's shoulder. 'I damn well hope so. I really do. You scared the dickens out of me when you drew that bow and fired that arrow. Damned if I know how you hit that rat.'

'I can see in the dark,' Iron Eyes explained.

'Have you always lived in that forest, boy?' the blacksmith wondered. 'How could you have survived when you was little?'

Iron Eyes pushed his long hair off his face. 'The

wolves looked after me until I was able to fend for myself. They still protect me when I need help.'

'Wolves?' Hartson swallowed hard.

Before Iron Eyes could reply the sound of loud voices drew his attention to the large barn doors. Men were approaching the livery stable unannounced.

The honed instincts of the young hunter immediately burst into action. His bullet-coloured eyes flashed at his drinking pal and then at the street.

Hartson again witnessed the unimaginable speed of his companion as Iron Eyes primed his bow with a fresh arrow, leapt to his feet and aimed straight at the sun-bleached barn doors.

'Men come,' he snarled.

FIVE

The two burly lumberjacks walked out of the blinding sunlight and into the livery. They were greeted by an arrow which took one of their hats clean off. The fatter of the pair stared up at his hat pinned to the barn door as his equally rotund friend glared at the archer who had swiftly placed another deadly arrow on his bowstring and was aiming it straight at them.

'Oh hell,' the first lumberjack stammered as he caught sight of Iron Eyes.

'Look what that bastard done to my brand new derby,' the other complained as he released his hat from where it was pinned. With a look of horror etched into his eyes, the logger threw the arrow at the ground and then glared at his prized derby hat with the holes in its bowl. 'What's going on here?'

His equally robust friend patted at his friend's gut as he stared across the livery at Iron Eyes who had another of his lethal missiles aimed at them.

42

'I'd hush the hell up if I was you,' he warned.

'Look at my hat,' the snorting lumberjack was almost in tears as he poked fingers through the fabric. 'It's ruined. My best hat has bin ruined.'

'Hush up before you end up in worse condition than your hat, buddy.' His pal finally managed to get his fellow logger to look to where he was pointing.

The irate man suddenly fell silent as he too spotted the fearful creature that had them in his sights. Both large figures were glued to the spot in sheer terror by the sight of the archer.

Neither had ever seen anything like the emaciated Iron Eyes as he held the bow in his bony hands and trained the flint arrowhead at them. It was impossible to see the face of the youngster as his long hair covered his determined features like a mask. But Iron Eyes could see them clearly enough as he gripped the bow firmly and held the arrow on the taut bowstring.

'What the hell is that?' one of the loggers stammered.

'Whatever it is,' the other said. 'He's sure got us where he wants us.'

They stared in utter disbelief at the horrific sight before them. Neither dared to move a muscle as they watched the young hunter standing in the centre of the livery close to where Bo Hartson was seated.

The blacksmith waved a hand at the lumberjacks.

'Howdy, boys,' he said. 'This is Iron Eyes.'

There were few things more terrifying than the

sight of the deathly Iron Eyes as he trained the bow
and arrow on them and glared from behind the veil
of long lifeless black hair.

'I reckon you spooked him,' Hartson added.

'What kinda name is Iron Eyes?' one of the loggers
asked his companion from the corner of his mouth.

'Me Iron Eyes,' the skeletal archer growled.

Both men wanted to turn and run but realized
that nobody could outrun an arrow in flight. Their
feet shuffled as the blacksmith took a sip from his tin
cup and tapped the leg of his tall young pal.

'Don't go killing them, boy,' he said as the satisfying liquor burned down his throat on its way to his
belly. 'I know them fat varmints.'

Iron Eyes looked disappointed. 'Are you sure?'

The blacksmith laughed and nodded.

'I'm sure, Iron Eyes,' he sighed.

'Listen to Bo, boy,' the lumberjack begged.

'We don't mean you no harm,' the other
exclaimed with equal terror in his voice. 'We just
come to give old Bo his winnings.'

Iron Eyes frowned as he stared through the limp
strands of hair that covered his face. He could sense
that the men were frightened but did not understand
what they were actually saying. He swiftly glanced at
the blacksmith as Hartson slowly got to his feet and
moved toward him.

'What they mean?' Iron Eyes asked as he kept the
bow string taut and aimed at his targets. 'What is winnings?'

44

Hartson placed a massive hand on the bony shoulder of the young hunter and whispered in Iron Eyes' ear.

'I won money on that prize fight, boy,' he explained as he carefully placed a hand on the youngster's outheld arm and slowly lowered the bow until it was aimed at the sod. 'This is just Luke and Charlie bringing me my winnings.'

Utterly bemused, Iron Eyes turned and stared straight into his friend's face and repeated his question. 'What is winnings?'

Hartson rolled his eyes and then recalled that Iron Eyes did not understand the ways of his civilized neighbours. The blacksmith rubbed the sweat from his face and indicated with a nod of his head for both the lumberjacks to advance.

'You know about dollars, huh?' he said to the hunter.

Iron Eyes pulled the arrow from the bow and slid it back into the leather pouch on his hip and nodded. 'I know. Dollars buy whiskey and cigars. Dollars good.'

'That's right, boy,' Hartson chuckled as both Luke and Charlie cautiously moved up beside the forge. 'I used some of my dollars to bet on the winner of the prize fight. I won so the boys here have brung me my winnings. More dollars.'

Iron Eyes watched as Luke Hardy handed the silver coins to the blacksmith as he and his pal both stared at the unusual youngster who towered over them all.

'You won dollars?' The gaunt youth repeated the still abstract thought. 'What if you had chosen the wrong fighter, Bo?'

'I'd have lost my money,' Hartson shrugged.

The youngster gave a disapproving shrug.

'Not good,' Iron Eyes shook his head as he hung the bow over his shoulder again and turned to face the still frightened lumberjacks. His uncanny eyes inspected both men carefully before returning to Hartson. 'Why risk your dollars? Dollars get whiskey and cigars.'

Luke Hardy turned to his fellow lumberjack Charlie Knox and shrugged. 'This skinny varmint is right. Betting is plumb loco when you weighs it up, ain't it?'

'Plumb loco and no mistake,' Knox agreed.

'How much did you bet on that fight, Charlie?' Hartson asked the well-built man. 'Tell my tall pal how many dollars you risked betting on that fight.'

'Ten dollars,' the lumberjack replied.

'I bet five,' Knox chipped in as he stared at the tall Iron Eyes carefully in his ill-fitting clothes.

'Did you boys win?' Hartson rubbed his whiskers.

'Nope,' the both replied at exactly the same time.

'You all loco,' Iron Eyes stated before checking the pelts hanging from his belt for the umpteenth time and then without a word of warning started walking toward the bright street.

'Where you going, Iron Eyes?' Hartson called out to the wide back of the hunter. 'I got another bottle of whiskey hid under the forge.'

Iron Eyes glanced back at the three men but continued walking out of the livery. 'Me trade furs for dollars and buy cigars and whiskey. I come back.'

As the tall emaciated figure walked out into the sun-baked street, the lumberjacks moved closer to the owner of the livery like a pair of vultures around a carcass.

'Crack that bottle open, Bo,' Charlie rubbed his hands together. 'I'm as dry as the desert and spitting up cactus.'

Luke Hardy stared to where he had last seen Iron Eyes and then tapped the arm of the blacksmith several times until he drew Hartson's attention.

'Who in tarnation is that critter, Bo?' he asked nervously, as though still fearful of being overheard by the stranger who had nearly unleashed his arrows at them. 'I've seen a lot of folks in this territory, but I ain't ever seen one that looked anything like him. He kinda troubles me.'

Knox looked at his fellow lumberjack and nodded in agreement. 'To be honest that boy kinda scares me as well, Bo. Who is he?'

Hartson lowered his ample bulk back on to the barrel and pulled out another bottle of whiskey from under the forge. He pulled its cork and spat it at the coals.

'That, my friends, is Iron Eyes,' the blacksmith said as he stared at the bottle in his hands. 'He's from the forest down yonder.'

Both men stared down at the seated blacksmith.

'Iron Eyes?' Charlie repeated the name. 'What kinda handle is that?'

Hartson looked up at the lumberjacks. 'That's what I call him, Charlie. He said his name was Ayan-Ees but I figured that was just what them Injuns in the forest call him. I figured it sounded like Iron Eyes, so that's what I've bin calling him. I've bin teaching him English.'

Luke sat down beside Hartson. 'You mean he just showed up here and couldn't talk?'

'That's about it,' the blacksmith nodded. 'He just wandered out of the forest one dark moonless night and I kinda took him under my wing.'

'Weird looking critter and no mistake,' Hardy spat at the sod floor and stared at the fresh bottle of whiskey in the hands of their host. 'What is he? He sure don't look exactly like a white man. Not with that long black mane of hair hanging halfway down his back.'

Hartson raised his eyebrows.

'Hell, that boy don't even know what he is,' he explained.

'He ain't no Injun,' Charlie Knox commented. 'He's way too tall to be an Injun.'

The blacksmith gestured to the lumberjacks to lower their voices as he glanced at the barn doors and then back at his guests.

'Don't go calling him an Injun, Charlie,' Hartson warned the lumberjacks. 'He gets real dangerous when folks imply that he's one. I found that out just before you boys showed up.'

'How come?' Luke wondered.

'Iron Eyes has spent his whole life in that forest dodging arrows,' the blacksmith began to explain. 'Them Injuns have bin trying to get his scalp since he was a runt.'

'Didn't he have no folks?' Knox questioned.

The blacksmith shook his head and sighed.

'Just wolves, Charlie,' Hartson repeated what Iron Eyes had told him. 'Iron Eyes was raised by timber wolves. If you seen him angry you'd know what I mean. Iron Eyes seems to turn into a wolf when he's riled.'

'Holy smoke,' Knox gulped.

'Gimme that,' Luke Hardy tore the whiskey bottle from Hartson's grip and took a big swig of the fiery liquor. He then handed it to his fellow lumberjack and watched as Charlie copied his action.

'Raised by wolves?' Knox stammered as he returned the bottle to the blacksmith and wiped his mouth along the back of his sleeve. 'That's what he reminded me of when he had that bow aimed at me and Luke. It was like looking into the eyes of a ravenous wolf.'

'I know what you mean,' Hartson nodded as he glanced at his friends. 'That's why I'm treating him with kid gloves, boys. Iron Eyes don't understand people like normal folks do and that's mighty dangerous.'

'Yeah, Iron Eyes don't understand nothing,' Hardy gulped nervously. 'You had to explain to him what "winnings" are, Bo. Iron Eyes might misunderstand some hombre in town and decide to rip the poor bastard to shreds or fill him with arrows.'

'At least he ain't toting a gun,' Knox sighed thankfully.

Hardy rubbed sweat from his brow.

'That kid would be plumb lethal if he got hold of a six-shooter, by my reckoning,' he said.

Charlie Knox loosened his bandanna. 'Luckily he's only got a bow and a pouch of arrows. If he tangles with anyone toting a Colt Peacemaker or the likes, he'll get his tail feathers shot off.'

The lumberjacks laughed, but the solemn blacksmith did not join in. He just rubbed his jaw with his thumbnail and brooded silently. Finally he leaned back and looked at both men in turn before speaking.

'There ain't nothing to be joshing about. Everything in Silver Creek is new to that boy,' Hartson warned as he took a long swallow of his whiskey. 'He's gonna make mistakes and for his sake I sure hope they ain't bad ones.'

'But he ain't got no guns,' Luke repeated.

The blacksmith took a swig from his whiskey bottle and then rested it on his knee. Sweat still rolled down his face from his sparse head of hair.

'Some folks don't need guns,' Hartson declared. 'Iron Eyes might be green when it comes to mixing it

50

with townsfolk, but I'd bet this livery stable that he could win any fight against anyone. That boy is what they call a feral child. Raised by wild critters until he actually is as wild as they are. If them Injuns ain't bin able to get the better of him, none of us in Silver Creek got a chance.'

Charlie Knox rubbed the sweat from his face and stared fearfully at the wide open barn doors. A shiver traced his spine and he shuddered.

'It's lucky there ain't no law in this town,' he said. 'I got me a feeling that Iron Eyes would fall foul of the law pretty damn quick.'

'But if he upsets the wrong folks in Silver Creek,' Luke added fearfully, 'They'll surely lynch him. Folks around here ain't the forgiving type.'

'They might try to lynch him,' Bo Hartson sighed heavily and reloaded his pipe bowl thoughtfully. 'But I got me a feeling that Iron Eyes ain't the sort to die easy, boys.'

'You reckon?' Charlie asked. 'We've seen half a dozen folks getting their necks stretched by the mobs around here, Bo. And none of them looked or acted anything like Iron Eyes.'

Hardy shrugged. 'Charlie's right. There's a lot of loud-mouthed bullies in Silver Creek that'd kill anyone just for looking different. You gotta admit it, Iron Eyes sure looks different and some folks get scared by things like that.'

Hartson gave a wry smile. His eyes twinkled at the thought of anyone trying to get the better of the unusual young hunter.

'A forest full of Injuns ain't managed it yet, have they?' Hartson struck a match and raised it to his pipe. 'I just hope and pray that nobody riles that youngster. God only knows what would happen if they riled him.'

'But nearly every varmint in Silver Creek got guns, Bo,' Charlie argued. 'Iron Eyes is just a kid. If they aim them guns in his direction, the boy's a gonner.'

'Are you sure about that?' Smoke billowed from his mouth before the blacksmith blew the match flame out and tossed the blackened ember at the forge.

For the first time since they had entered the large wooden structure, both the burly lumberjacks were silent. Even though every ounce of logic they had thrown at their muscular friend seemed to say that the naïve youngster had little if any chance of bettering the heavily armed menfolk in Silver Creek, they knew Hartson was probably right.

Iron Eyes looked young and scrawny, but he also looked like someone who indeed would not die easily.

SIX

Three of the powerfully-built lumberjacks had been making the most of their first day off from felling trees in over a month. They had been drinking steadily since before sunrise and had been causing trouble for the last hour as they moved between the numerous saloons in Silver Creek.

The trio of large men were well known in the remote logging town for causing trouble. It seemed that the more hard liquor they consumed, the more infamous they became. Hog Barker was the self-proclaimed leader of the bunch. He was a humourless soul who never failed to get even more so when he was drinking whiskey. Drew Smith was a bitter character who carried a chip on his shoulder which was as big as a giant redwood. He had already killed three men in the territory for various reasons and intended to add to his tally. Like Barker, Smith could not hold his liquor and grew meaner with every sip of the powerful whiskey.

Both men had each downed at least two bottles of rotgut since they had started drinking that morning. They were like so many of their kind in the logging wilderness and hated anyone they deemed different to themselves. To them, all men who they considered to be better looking than themselves were fair game. They would taunt and mock until their chosen target got angry enough to react and then proceed to beat the person up. The largest and quietest of the three was a lumbering soul known as Shake Norris.

Norris was a man of few words and even fewer friends. He would work harder than most and do what other folks told him to do. Norris might have been the biggest of the bunch and probably the strongest, but he was basically not a man who ever started a fight.

Yet like so many others, Norris was easily led. He tended to tag along with Barker and Smith like a faithful hound dog so that he could convince himself that he had friends.

In truth, Barker and Smith only wanted Norris in their company because his sheer size frightened those who might give them trouble.

As the three men left the Tall Tree saloon, they caught sight of the unusual sight of Iron Eyes as he made his way toward the hardware store to sell his furs. For some reason, the sight of the tall lean figure seemed to anger both Hog Barker and Smith.

His youth angered them because it reminded both loggers of their own advancing years. His pitifully lean form drew them like a magnet for they knew that most men built the way that Iron Eyes was built were very easy to beat to a bloody pulp.

But the main thing that had caught their attention was the mane of long black hair which hung impressively on Iron Eyes' wide shoulders.

Hatred for Indians of any type had been instilled in both the lumberjacks from childhood. Like so many men of their generation they truly believed that the only good Indian was a dead Indian.

Besides, you could kill Indians in practically any of the states and territories without ever being charged with murder. It seemed that even the law was blind when it came to people of a certain colour.

Barker and Smith watched from across the wide street as the tall hunter headed to the hardware store to trade his furs for goods. They kept pace with Iron Eyes as Norris tagged behind them as usual.

'Who is that weird looking critter, Hog?' Smith asked as he shared a bottle of whiskey with the older lumberjack. 'What's he doing in Silver Creek?'

Barker grew angrier the longer he cast his evil stare upon the tall youngster. 'I don't know who that varmint is but he don't belong here. We're gonna have to teach him that we don't like Injuns in our town.'

Smith started to chuckle as they continued to keep level with Iron Eyes on the opposite boardwalk. He turned and looked at the lumbering Norris.

'You ready to stomp on an Injun, Shake?' he asked

his bigger friend. 'Stomp him into pulp.'

Norris gave a nod of his head and continued to trail his two companions. As always he followed their lead.

The afternoon heat showed no sign of easing up across the high clearing where Silver Creek stood. The sun beat down mercilessly upon the weathered structures that had served for years as a home for its cast of misfits gathered between its unmarked borders. The various aromas common in such places grew even stronger as the lean figure of the hunter made his way along the wide street. Yet he either did not notice the stench of numerous outhouses in need of lime, or his mind was on something else.

The thought of getting his hands on strong cigars and cheap whiskey filled the youngster's every thought. Nothing else mattered to the stranger as he made his way along the boardwalk to the general store.

Iron Eyes looked baffled by the sight in and around Silver Creek as he strode on. The sandy ground of the street showed all the signs of a place where the brutal prize fight had just occurred only a half hour earlier.

Blood, teeth and lumps of scarlet gore littered the sand where the two mountainous men had battered one another to a pulp to earn themselves a few dollars and entertain the baying crowd.

The sand at the exact spot where the street had

been roped off was stained a sickening shade of red. There was no mistake what had occurred there, Iron Eyes thought as he passed by the hideous evidence.

Yet no matter how hard he tried, Iron Eyes still could not understand the reason why grown men would fight this way. It made no sense to him as he stepped down and strode across the sandy ground to the boardwalk outside the large store.

He had grown up in what these people regarded as the wilderness, but Iron Eyes knew that none of the forest's inhabitants would ever indulge in such acts. Not even the most vicious of wild beasts would fight for the sake of fighting.

Although he loathed the Indians who had stalked him for his entire life, Iron Eyes had never seen any of their warriors engage in any similar pointless actions.

In the forest animals of every kind might use their prowess to establish their superiority over rivals, but that was as far as it went. They killed for food and never wasted an ounce of energy on anything else.

Iron Eyes mounted the store's steps and moved up toward the shade of the porch overhang. As his hand reached toward the door knob of the general store, he heard the sound of blatant laughter behind his broad back.

He stopped and turned.

His eyes squinted hard until they were almost shut.

His long black hair swayed in the afternoon breeze that travelled along the dry shimmering street. Then he saw the large men on the opposite side of the street. Three men were standing outside one of the many saloons dotted along the wide street and they were looking directly at him.

Iron Eyes could not tell what they were calling out between their laughing, but he instinctively knew that they were not being complimentary.

It was obvious even to the naïve Iron Eyes that they were mocking him for some reason. He could not understand it, but the gaunt youngster grew no less angry.

Kermit Lang, the owner of the store, was known to the youngster and had purchased several furs from Iron Eyes on his previous visits. He opened the store door and moved beside the tall figure. He held his broom in his small hands and brushed the dust off the boardwalk.

The old man knew exactly what the intention of the three lumberjacks was. He had seen Hog Barker and Drew Smith taunt many less physically capable men before. He had also seen Smith gun down an innocent drummer in the street just for the sheer pleasure of it.

'Don't pay them no mind, Iron Eyes,' Lang said as he brushed the sand off the edge of the boards in a vain attempt to stem the tide of dust that perpetually made its way into his store. 'They're drunk and probably lost most of their money betting on the loser of the prize fight. Get in here.'

Iron Eyes tilted his head and glanced at the store-keeper before returning his terrifying attention to the loud men opposite.

'Men angry?' he asked Lang.

'Yep,' Lang nodded and shrugged his ancient shoulders as he turned and started back into his store. 'Men like that bunch are always angry, Iron Eyes.'

Iron Eyes spun on his heels and trailed the older soul into the general store. He was confused by the fact that men that he had never encountered before would obviously try and rile him. He closed the door behind him and walked after the older man.

'Why they shout at me?' he asked Lang as the older man rested his hands on the counter of his store. 'They do not know me.'

Lang sighed and rolled his eyes.

'They're liquored up,' Lang said. 'They seen you and they figure that they'll feel a whole lot better if they can lure you into a fight and beat the tar out of you.'

'Beat the tar?' Iron Eyes repeated the words but did not understand what Lang was getting at. 'Why they want to fight Iron Eyes, Kerm? Not even the dumbest critter in forest picks a fight for no reason.'

Lang smile from behind his trimmed white moustache.

'They figure that you're a tad scrawny, son,' Lang said as he glanced through his large glass windows at the drunken trio on the other side of the street. 'Men like them are always on the lookout for critters they can best in a fight. Beating folks up makes them feel

59

bigger, I guess.'

Iron Eyes shook his head. He did not understand.

Lang leaned closer to the tall hunter.

'I got me a saying,' he chuckled. 'The smallest dogs always bark the loudest. Big old hound dogs don't have to bark coz they already know that they don't have to prove themselves.'

Iron Eyes understood the words and grinned. 'You give dollars for my furs, Kerm?'

'Top dollar,' Lang added as he accepted the furs and studied them carefully. 'You want dollars or goods?'

Iron Eyes looked at the small storekeeper, 'Whiskey and cigars. Dollars no good in forest.'

Lang brushed the pelts and blew at the furs before carefully hanging them up behind the counter. He then studied the tall youth with seasoned understanding. He pulled out a box of cigars and handed them to Iron Eyes and then reached down under the counter and produced a few bottles of whiskey.

'That should make us even, Iron Eyes,' he said. 'Agreed?'

'Iron Eyes happy,' the tall figure said as he went to gather up his goods. He stopped when he spied the three lumberjacks. They had crossed the street and were now standing on the boardwalk outside the double windowed store. Hog Barker banged on the window.

'Git on out here, freak,' he shouted.

'What they want?' Iron Eyes whispered as his narrowed eyes darted between the three figures. 'I do not know them. Why they want me out there?'

Lang reached across his store counter and caught hold of his tall friend's arm. He drew Iron Eyes' attention.

'You can use the door at the rear of the store if you like, Iron Eyes,' he suggested. 'They'll surely hurt you if you go out front.'

Iron Eyes glanced at Lang for a heartbeat.

'Why?' he wondered. 'I do not savvy.'

'Them boys are out to hurt you,' Lang informed as he sighed. 'Cut out the back way and you could probably outrun them drunkards.'

'I no run away from fools, Kerm,' the tall man growled.

'You'll get yourself pistol-whipped, boy,' Lang warned as he noticed Iron Eyes starting to pull his Indian bow from his shoulder while staring with unblinking eyes at the trio of hefty lumberjacks standing on the store's boardwalk. 'Listen to me. There ain't no glory in getting your brains knocked out by mindless thugs.'

Iron Eyes looked at the storekeeper with a puzzled expression etched on his face. He placed his bow on the shop counter and then unhooked his quiver of deadly arrows from his crude belt. He laid the arrows next to the arrows and nodded at Lang.

'Guard my weapons and goods, Kerm,' he muttered before returning his terrifying glare to the men gathered like rabid hounds beneath the porch over-hang. 'This should not take too long.'

'Don't go out there, Iron Eyes,' Lang begged the tall youngster. 'They're armed. They got guns and you ain't. They'll slaughter you.'

'I no need guns,' Iron Eyes said.

'Trust me, Iron Eyes,' Lang pleaded. 'Even if you did manage to best them with your fists, they'll shoot you down like a dog.'

'Iron Eyes is not a dog, Kerm,' he grinned. 'I am a wolf, though.'

Kermit Lang did not know whether Iron Eyes was brave or just plain stupid as the young hunter calmly started for the door.

'Where are you going, boy?' the storekeeper asked.

Iron Eyes paused and shook his long hair off his face as he looked at the old man with the troubled expression etched into his ancient features.

'I go to slaughter them,' he muttered before start-ing for the door again. 'I am the hunter. I am Iron Eyes.'

Lang sank his face into the palms of his hands.

He could not look.

SEVEN

Kermit Lang could not bear to watch. He listened to the door handle being turned and then peeked through his fingers as Iron Eyes stepped out on to the porch and then stopped between the three large loggers. The storekeeper clenched his fists and then rested them on the store counter as he heard Iron Eyes start to speak.

'What you men want of Iron Eyes?' the emaciated youngster asked as his head lowered and his mane of hair covered his face from the lumberjacks' curious eyes. 'I want no trouble. Go now.'

Hog Barker burst into laughter at the painfully thin youngster's words. 'Listen to the skinny bastard, boys. He wants us to go. I reckon that's a warning.'

'I'm thirsty, Hog,' Norris said as he rested a shoulder on the wooden upright at the end of the boardwalk. 'Let's go and find us some rotgut whiskey. This critter ain't worth bothering with.'

Barker glanced at the biggest of the lumberjacks.

'Hush up, Shake,' he snorted. 'This long bean-pole needs to be teached a lesson. I don't hanker being ordered about by a stinking Injun.'

Iron Eyes felt his blood starting to boil as it flowed through his veins. He snorted angrily.

'I am no Injun,' he hissed through his gritted teeth.

Barker moved to directly before Iron Eyes and laughed out loud at the motionless young hunter. He jabbed his fingers into the chest of the youngster.

'Reckon we struck a nerve there, boys,' the logger chuckled as he eyed the painfully lean man. 'He don't like being called an Injun. Hell, no white *hombre* ever looked like that.'

Iron Eyes lowered his head like a bull contemplating a charge a matador's cape. His fiery stare burned across the distance between them.

'You leave Iron Eyes alone and go away now,' he snarled as his fists clenched at his sides.

Only two of the big men were amused by the words that came spitting from the mouth of Iron Eyes. Shake Norris remained at the end of the boardwalk silently watching the events unfurl. Unlike Barker and Smith, the largest of the lumberjacks was nowhere near as confident as them. He sensed that there was more to the long-haired stranger than met the eye. He could tell that the youngster was like a powder keg and about to explode into action.

'Look at him, boys,' Hog Barker shouted as he rested his shoulder against the wooden upright and stared at the unusual vision before him. 'He sure is a pitiful sight to behold and no mistake.'

'All Injuns are pitiful, Hog,' Smith grunted.

A strange new sensation swept over Iron Eyes as he stood between the burly men. He could not understand why he felt so angry because it was an emotion that was totally alien to him. He had never before been mocked or taunted by anyone and that did not sit well with him.

'I tell you again,' Iron Eyes growled. 'I am not Injun.'

'You sure smell like one,' Barker laughed.

Iron Eyes tilted his head and stared through his mane of sweat-soaked locks at Barker. He remained totally still as he listened to Shake Norris move at the end of the boardwalk. He then cast his bullet-coloured eyes at the third logger. Drew Smith was probably the most dangerous of the bunch and continually stroked his holstered gun grip.

'He talks mighty big for a stinking Injun, Hog,' Smith commented. 'We should teach him a lesson that it don't pay to talk back to his betters.'

'You could be right, Drew,' Barker grinned. 'We should pistol whip the freak and then tie him to a horse and drag his sorrowful hide around town. That should do the trick.'

Silently, Iron Eyes inhaled deeply. He was like a volcano getting ready to erupt into unimaginable ferocity. His eyes continued to watch them through the limp strands of his hair.

'Can't you talk, scarecrow?' Barker shouted before edging away from the wooden upright and moving toward the silent young hunter. 'Look at you, boy. What kinda gear are you wearing? No white man wears clothes like that. You're just pathetic. Ain't you ashamed of being in the same town as real men, boy?'

Smith and Norris moved closer to Iron Eyes as he absorbed the venomous insults that Barker was dishing out at him. The tall hunter continued to listen to the boards creak under their boots as they surrounded him.

Barker grabbed at Iron Eyes' long hair and twisted it in his large hand like a mangle. Yet no matter how much the logger twisted the hair, Iron Eyes showed no reaction.

'Cat got your tongue, boy?' he screamed at Iron Eyes, but he still did not react to the lumberjacks.

Barker released his grip of the greasy mane and then rubbed the palm of his hand down his shirt. Although none of them could actually see Iron Eyes' face, the gaunt hunter observed them clearly from behind the veil of limp matted strands.

'Maybe he's gone mute, Hog,' Smith laughed.

'He sure is quiet,' Barker rocked with laughter.

'I got me a feeling he's one of them Injuns we've seen up in the forest,' Smith boomed.

Finally Iron Eyes was through being insulted and mocked by the men who insisted on calling him by the name of those who had been trying to kill him for all of his days. He straightened up to his full height and shook the hair off his face and stared at them in turn with cold calculating eyes.

His adversaries stopped in their tracks as they caught sight of his hardened features. Iron Eyes no longer looked as vulnerable as he had when they first saw him. Now Iron Eyes looked as lethal as he truly was.

He glared at them in turn.

'Go away or I will kill you,' he warned.

The lumberjacks were startled, yet only Norris backed away to the side of the general store. He alone was smart enough to realize that Iron Eyes was not merely warning them, he was making a prophecy.

'Let's get out of here, boys,' he urged nervously. 'That critter means it. He's gonna kill us.'

Iron Eyes raised his hands and pushed his hair off his face. His unblinking stare glared at Smith and Barker in turn in the same way that he always looked at his chosen prey.

'Listen to big man,' he hissed like a sidewinder at Barker and Smith. 'He is smart. I will kill you.'

'Shake ain't smart,' Barker shook his head and spat at Iron Eyes. 'He's just gutless.'

The gaunt hunter wiped the spittle from his face and then began to growl like a wild beast. Every sinew in his lean body shook as his eyes darted between Barker and Smith.

Hog Barker looked hard at Iron Eyes as though suddenly aware that this misfit might not be quite as easily beaten as they had first imagined. His hand moved toward his holstered six-shooter.

'I'm gonna bust you into little bits, kid,' he vowed before shaking his fist at the tall young hunter. 'No freak of nature ever got the better of me and I don't intend letting you be the first. You're the one that's gonna die.'

'Let's kill him, Hog,' Smith said threateningly.

Barker nodded angrily.

'You're a dead man,' he started jabbing a massive digit in the air between himself and Iron Eyes. Each movement was followed by words designed to make the emotionless young hunter react and rush him. 'You are the dumbest critter I ever set eyes on.'

Iron Eyes said nothing.

Barker snarled. 'You ain't nothing but a stinking Injun trying to look like regular folks. It don't work, boy. We can smell you just like we can smell your kinfolk back in them trees. It ain't no crime in this territory to kill an Injun.'

'Hell, you're already a dead man,' Smith joshed as he too started to poke at the air with his own finger. 'We'd be doing you a favour by killing you.'

Iron Eyes took a step forward.

'I am no Injun,' the emaciated hunter spat. 'I am Iron Eyes the wolf.'

Smith and Barker clutched their bellies as they rocked with laughter.

'You're plumb loco, boy,' Barker laughed. 'You really think that you're a wolf?'

'He's loco all right,' Smith joked. 'Must have got his brains kicked out by an ornery mule. We'd best shoot the varmint now before he starts howling.'

Iron Eyes started to breathe long and hard.

'Let's leave this fella be, boys,' Norris said. 'I got me a real bad feeling about the scrawny critter.'

Barker's eyebrows rose in astonishment when he heard his friend's words. He glanced at the larger of the loggers and laughed.

'You reckon that this skinny Injun can get the better of us, Shake?' he asked before pulling his six-shooter from its holster and waving it under the nose of Iron Eyes. 'Watch what he does when I blow his head off his shoulders.'

Norris looked even more concerned.

'Yep, I'm scared, boys. I got me a feeling that he's way more dangerous than he looks,' Norris nodded firmly. 'Let's go back to the saloon and do us some more drinking, Hog.'

Smith rallied next to Barker.

'Don't go listening to Shake, Hog,' he urged. 'He ain't even toting a gun. We got to teach this stinking Injun a lesson or before we know what's happening Silver Creek will be full of them.'

Hog Barker screwed up his face and nodded.

'Damn right, Drew,' he stepped forward with his six-gun aimed straight at Iron Eyes. 'I'm gonna kill this bastard so none of his kind dare show their faces in Silver Creek ever again.'

The words had barely left the lumberjack's mouth

when Iron Eyes sprang into action. His left forearm fanned and knocked the gun barrel aside. He then smashed his right fist into the face of the far bulkier man. As Barker staggered back, Iron Eyes kicked out and caught Smith in his belly. He then lowered his head and ran like a raging bull into the surprised Barker.

Iron Eyes hit the logger with all his might.

Both he and Barker flew off the boardwalk and crashed through the hitching pole a few feet below. Splinters rose up into the air from the shattered remnants of the pole and showered over the scene before they collided with the unforgiving ground. Barker landed on his back amid the debris as the hunter bounced off the logger's ample girth.

Iron Eyes somersaulted over the winded Barker and landed on his feet. He kicked the six-shooter from Barker's hand and glanced at Smith dragging his own gun from his holster.

Barker groaned and attempted to rise.

Iron Eyes kicked the logger in the jaw and then, as teeth and blood splattered in all directions, he felt the heat of a bullet pass within inches of his leg. The hunter spun around and looked up at Smith on the boardwalk holding his freshly discharged weapon in his hand.

Iron Eyes gave out a guttural growl.

Smith fired another shot at Iron Eyes. The bullet flew over his head. The young hunter narrowed his bullet-coloured eyes as a fevered rage enveloped him.

Iron Eyes charged.

In three long strides his agile body had mounted a water trough and leapt on to the boardwalk. He caught Smith around the waist and knocked the logger off his feet. Both men crashed on to the boardwalk. Dust rose around the men as Smith desperately tried to cock his six-gun again while the lean hunter grappled with the far heavier man.

Iron Eyes was no match for the far bulkier logger. He was tossed around mercilessly but hung on doggedly. As they wrestled Iron Eyes realized that the far stronger man still had his six-shooter in his hand.

No matter how hard the younger man tried, he could not stop Smith from dragging back on his gun hammer. The sound of the smoking weapon being cocked alerted Iron Eyes that the logger was far from finished.

Both men rolled over and over in a frenzied battle to get the upper hand. Although the lumberjack was far more powerful, the emaciated youngster was more agile. He twisted and turned and kept punching Smith's face at every opportunity as they rolled across the boardwalk.

Knowing that his life depended upon it, Iron Eyes' bony left hand firmly gripped Smith's wrist in an attempt to stop the lumberjack from firing the gun again.

Then Smith smashed a powerful fist into his foe's jaw.

The power of the punch rocked Iron Eyes' head.

A lightning bolt exploded inside his skull as he fell stunned on to his face.

Blood filled his throat and came sputtering out of his mouth as he turned his head. Iron Eyes watched the crimson pool grow beside his open mouth. Then before he had time to gather his dazed thoughts he felt the hot steel barrel of Smith's .45 press against his temple.

'You fight pretty good for a skinny bastard,' Smith snarled into the hunter's ear.

The feel of the metal against his skull dragged Iron Eyes out of his stupor. Faster than he had ever moved before, he raised his hand and hit the six-shooter away just as Smith squeezed its trigger.

The sound was deafening. Heat from the blinding flash burned Iron Eyes' cheekbone as the bullet passed within inches of the long-legged hunter. Racked by pain, Iron Eyes scrambled back to his feet just as Smith swung his left fist at him venomously. The logger's powerful punch narrowly missed the younger man's jaw as Iron Eyes stumbled against the large store window.

Before Iron Eyes could steady himself the lumber-jack threw his superior bulk at the still dazed hunter. The horrendous sound of breaking glass filled the entire town as both men went crashing through one of the store's windows.

EIGHT

Frantically, both men kept smashing their fists into one another as they crashed through the tall window and flew through the air. Drew Smith had caught his tall opponent around the middle and sent them both stumbling backward through the large window. A thousand shards of glass hit the interior of the store as Iron Eyes and Smith landed heavily on the floor-boards. Even as both men fought feverishly on the ground, glass daggers landed on and around them.

Smith arched his back as he was peppered with the dangerous debris from the window. Yet even as chunks of glass hit the logger, he continued to try and better the youngster beneath him. He thrashed the gun hammer at his opponent's head, but the stunned young hunter managed to avoid the hot six-shooter.

Iron Eyes grabbed at Smith's face and clawed at the far heavier man's eyes in an attempt to make the lumberjack get off him. It was a desperate act but Iron Eyes knew that if he did not get Smith off him soon, the gun would smash his skull into fragments.

Finally Smith pulled back and allowed Iron Eyes to escape from under him. The youngster grabbed the wrist of his foe and jerked it backward into Smith's face. The body of the gun caught the logger across the bridge of his nose.

Pain rocked the big man as he felt the bones in his face shatter. Smith rocked on his knees as Iron Eyes slid out from under him. The youngster threw himself at the lumberjack, caught Smith around his muscular shoulders and sent him flying on to his back. Slivers of glass fell from the flesh of both men as they wrestled on the ground. Blood seeped from the numerous wounds of both men as they continued to blindly fight.

It was like two rutting stags battling for supremacy.

Neither was willing to quit. They both knew that to do so was to die. They traded blows and knocked one another through the store to the store-keeper's horror.

'Quit that,' Kermit Lang screamed as he watched his store being turned to matchwood before his eyes. 'Get the hell out of here before you wreck the place.'

The words fell on deaf ears. Neither Smith nor Iron Eyes could hear anything apart from the sound of the store being demolished around them. Iron Eyes could see the six-gun in Smith's hand trying to get a bead on his painfully lean frame and doing everything he could to avoid the lethal weapon.

Iron Eyes leapt with the agility of a puma over one of the store-keeper's display stands, landed behind it and then pushed the entire thing over Smith as the logger lumbered toward it.

Goods crashed on top of the far larger man. Everything from lanterns to candlesticks cascaded on to the lumberjack as he wiped the blood from his jaw and tried to see his elusive prey.

'Stop it, you mindless fools,' Lang screamed out at the top of his voice. It was pointless though. Neither Smith nor Iron Eyes could hear anything apart from their own grunts.

As the large wooden stand broke into a dozen pieces, Iron Eyes jumped at Smith. Both men hit the floorboards hard, but it was the youngster who scrambled to his feet first.

Panting heavily, Iron Eyes saw Smith dragging back on his gun hammer again. Before the logger had time to raise the gun and fire, the athletic youngster leapt through the shattered window on to the boardwalk.

Iron Eyes landed on his hands and rolled over until he was in a crouching position. He swung around and watched as Smith came crashing back out after him like a real ornery grizzly.

Not waiting for Smith to fire his gun again, Iron Eyes charged into the lumberjack with every scrap of strength that he could muster. His head hit Smith in his belly and stopped the far larger man in his tracks.

But Smith did not topple over. The logger simply watched as Iron Eyes bounced off his ample girth.

Suddenly the six-gun fired.

The shot went between Iron Eyes' thin legs and took a chunk of the boardwalk off the ground. Iron Eyes let out a bone-chilling growl and leapt to his feet. His bullet-coloured eyes glared at Smith as he plucked shards of glass from his blood-soaked shirt.

'Big mistake, fat man,' he snarled.

'What you call me, runt?' smith raged.

Iron Eyes was through talking. He flew through the air at Smith like a whirlwind. The six-gun erupted again into deafening fury. The bullet missed the thin body of the youngster.

Drew Smith was as weary as the blood-soaked youngster. He fired his gun at his evasive target but missed Iron Eyes by at least a foot.

'Stand still, you yella bastard,' the logger gasped.

Iron Eyes rubbed the scarlet gore off his face and fought to remain on his tired legs. Every ounce of his honed instincts told him that the brutal battle was near an end and all he had to do was stay alive for a little longer.

'Stand still,' Smith yelled as he dragged his gun hammer back again. 'I wanna kill you clean.'

It was obvious that the lumberjack was deadly serious and wanted to put an end to Iron Eyes with one clean shot of his smoking .45. Moving back and forth across the boardwalk, Iron Eyes arched in agony as the six-shooter spewed out another bullet.

The tall youngster winced as he felt the bullet as it cut a trail across his ribs. He staggered and glared at Smith. His hand grabbed at his side and then he noticed the blood trickling from between his bony fingers.

Iron Eyes could not understand why the lumberjack did not fire again and finish him. He stared at the bleeding Smith and waited for the logger to finish him off.

But Drew Smith had no bullets left in the chambers of his smoking gun, only spent casings. Smith laughed like a madman at Iron Eyes. The hunter swayed on to his boots and cradled his side with his hand. His bullet-coloured eyes focused through the gunsmoke at the laughing lumberjack.

'Did that hurt, Injun?' Smith taunted as he opened up his six-gun and shook the casings out.

Iron Eyes had no notion of how guns worked and did not understand what the lumberjack was doing as the bigger man started to pull fresh bullets from his gun-belt and started to reload.

'It hurt,' Iron Eyes spat.

'You're a dead Injun, boy,' Smith bellowed. 'Get ready to meet your Maker.'

Iron Eyes watched as Smith kept sliding bullets into the smoking belly of his firearm. His eyes narrowed.

'What you doing?' Iron Eyes asked curiously.

The question confused the logger. Smith paused and looked the wounded hunter in the eyes.

'I'm reloading my gun, you halfwit,' he said. 'Ain't you seen a man reloading his gun before?'

'Nope,' Iron Eyes shook his head as he cautiously moved closer to the man he intended killing. 'Not see guns before coming here.'

The statement caused Smith to fumble with the bullet he was about to slide into the gun chamber. He frowned.

'You ain't seen any guns before?' he repeated.

Iron Eyes shook his head.

A cruel smile carved its way across Smith's face as he snapped his gun shut and adjusted its ramrod. His thumb pulled back on his gun hammer and he began to grunt with laughter as he stared at the wounded young hunter before him.

'Reckon you're gonna die now, you skinny bastard,' he drawled mockingly.

But Smith would soon learn that Iron Eyes was not so easily killed. The tall youth grunted and growled like a cornered timber wolf as his savage survival instincts rose up within him.

'I don't die so easy,' he whispered.

NINE

Blood covered the sun-bleached boards all around the two very different creatures who faced one another on the store front. Smith's words rattled inside his head as Iron Eyes felt blood trailing down his side and the various other wounds that covered his skinny body. Every sinew of the elusive hunter sensed that death was closer than it had ever been before. Yet Iron Eyes was determined that he would not be the loser of this final fight.

He stared at the brutal Smith like a mountain lion studying its chosen target and let out a low growl.

'You are brave,' Iron Eyes mocked. 'I have no gun so I cannot be as brave as you.'

The expression on Smith's face altered.

'You got a smart mouth, boy,' he growled. 'Them teeth of yours are digging your grave, though.'

'Maybe,' Iron Eyes said as he shuffled from side to side in a hypnotic manner. 'Shoot me.'

Without warning, Iron Eyes bolted across the

boardwalk to its very edge and then jumped. His bony hands grabbed a wooden upright and swung his lightweight body out over the sand. The momentum increased as Iron Eyes came hurtling back toward his adversary. He released his grip and flew boot-first at the startled Smith. Both his boots caught the lumberjack high in his chest. The impact felt like a mule kick and buckled the sturdy lumberjack. Yet even that was not enough to knock Smith off his feet.

Smith staggered back for a few steps and then steadied himself as he raised his .45. He fired his six-gun at his elusive prey. The bullet went through the porch roof and showered both men with debris. Covered in falling dust, Iron Eyes lashed out with his left boot and caught the logger in his midriff. Pain etched Smith's face for a few moments as he stared at the defiant Iron Eyes.

'You shouldn't have done that,' he gasped.

Iron Eyes silently agreed with the words. His foot hurt where it had collided with Smith's belly. It was far harder than it looked. He narrowed his eyes and rubbed blood from his face.

Suddenly Smith charged into the pitifully lean hunter.

Iron Eyes was lifted off his boots as Smith charged into him. Both men staggered across the boardwalk until Iron Eyes succumbed to the lumberjack's weight and crashed on to the boards. Like a slippery eel, Iron Eyes slithered and squirmed beneath his adversary. As Smith started to rise, Iron Eyes grabbed one of the logger's legs and then tripped him over on to his face. Smith hit the ground heavily but managed to fire his gun again at the more agile Iron Eyes.

The bullet ripped through the back of Iron Eyes' shirt and grazed his flesh before exiting close to his mane of long black hair.

No branding iron could have inflicted more pain. It felt as though someone had set fire to his back as Iron Eyes grabbed the lumberjack and wrestled him into the wall of the general store.

The sound of their skulls colliding with the sturdy wall echoed along the porch. As blood trickled down his face Iron Eyes threw two punches and clambered to his feet. Half dazed, Smith snorted and got to his feet just as Iron Eyes stepped back and kicked him between his legs. Smith squealed like a cornered pig and then pushed Iron Eyes back.

The sheer force sent the taller man halfway down the boardwalk before he could steady himself. Iron Eyes was about to charge into Smith again when he heard the unmistakable sound of the six-shooter being cocked again.

'No more shooting,' he snarled and waved his left hand at the burly logger.

Smith might have laughed if he had not been nursing his crotch and trying to straighten himself back into an upright position. He glanced to where he had last seen Norris standing but the giant lumberjack was gone.

81

'Shake,' Smith yelled out.

Iron Eyes gritted his razor sharp teeth and shook his fist at the lumberjack. He was amused that Smith seemed to be looking for reinforcements.

'He run off when you started shooting,' Iron Eyes informed the big man. 'Him smart. He not want to die.'

'He's just a yella belly,' Smith snarled as he rested his back against the wall. 'Gutless.'

Iron Eyes could see that Smith was still in agony as he fearlessly squared up to him. The .45 was shaking in the logger's hand as he attempted to aim its smoking barrel at Iron Eyes.

'Big mistake, fat man,' the blood-soaked young hunter snarled. 'Big mistake.'

Smith forced a grin. 'You're just like all Injuns. You're a coward like Shake.'

Anger rippled through the young hunter. Iron Eyes gritted his teeth and hissed through them.

'I not Injun,' he repeated.

Smith eased himself away from the wall and took a couple of faltering steps until he was facing the wounded young hunter. He glanced down at the smoke still trailing from his gun barrel and then back at Iron Eyes.

'Whatever you are,' he started, 'you're gonna be dead pretty soon.'

Iron Eyes looked down at his right boot. He could see the hilt of his long knife tucked its neck. He knew that he had only one chance of survival and that meant using the lethal stiletto before Smith squeezed his trigger again.

'Are you ready to die now, Injun?' Smith spat.

'Iron Eyes ready,' Iron Eyes replied.

The lumberjack was grinning as he aimed straight at the lean figure. Then Iron Eyes bent forward and lowered his arm until his skeletal fingers found the handle of the knife.

'What you doing, Injun?' Smith snarled at the unusual sight before him. 'Straighten up, damn it.'

Suddenly Iron Eyes did exactly that. He pulled the knife free from the neck of his boot and propelled it at the lumberjack with every last drop of his strength. The dagger sped across the boardwalk and embedded into the centre of Smith's chest. The sound of the impact was like the beating of a war drum.

A solitary thud.

Never taking his eyes off the stricken lumberjack, Iron Eyes swayed and tried to remain upright. His burning stare focused on the hilt of his weapon sticking out of Smith's massive chest. The logger looked shocked as it suddenly dawned on him that he was dying.

'What the hell?' Smith exclaimed.

The mocking smile disappeared from Smith's face as blood began to rise up into his mouth and drip from the corners of his mouth. He exhaled and stared down at the knife buried up to its hilt in his shirt front.

The logger watched in stunned horror as blood

83

crept around the knife hilt and spread over his shirt.

The smoking gun fell from the logger's grip and bounced on the boardwalk. Bewildered, Smith looked up at his bleeding adversary in disbelief. He tried to speak but only crimson gore spluttered from his mouth.

Emotionless, Iron Eyes watched as the far bigger man fell on to his knees. The lumberjack's eyes darted all around the area as though seeking help, but he was beyond any form of help. All Smith could do was die.

Then he toppled on to his side.

A strange gurgling sound came from the logger's mouth and his eyes suddenly went blank. He then arched and sank into a deep sleep. It was a sleep that he would never awaken from.

A sleep only shared by the dead.

Iron Eyes pushed his long hair off his face and then sighed heavily before glancing down at the blood that was still pulsating from his side. He pressed his hand against the wound and then strode unsteadily toward the body of the lumberjack.

There was no sign of regret in what he had just done.

For Iron Eyes knew that when anything was trying to kill you, there was only one thing you could do, and that was to kill it first.

The gangly young hunter stared down at Smith and pointed at the dead man. He jabbed the air.

'I am Iron Eyes,' he snarled at the body before

reaching down and extracting the knife from Smith's chest. Blood clung to the long twelve-inch blade as he wiped it clean on his pants leg. 'I am not Injun.'

When satisfied that he had removed the warm blood from the razor sharp blade he slid it back into his boot neck and turned back toward the stores open doorway. Before Iron Eyes could take a step toward it, Kermit Lang came scurrying out on to the boardwalk and moved straight to the body.

Startled, Iron Eyes watched as the store-keeper checked the lumberjack's various pockets until he located what he was looking for.

'What you got there, Kerm?' the wounded youth asked the store-keeper.

Lang waved the bag of coins under Iron Eyes' nose.

'I got me his money, boy,' he replied. 'That bastard is gonna pay for the repairs on my store. Besides the undertaker would only steal it.'

Iron Eyes watched as the smaller man hurried back toward the open doorway. He was confused by Lang's words and actions as he turned to face him. Lang snapped his fingers and got the bleeding young hunter's attention.

'Are you coming in here?' he asked.

Iron Eyes gave a sharp nod of his head. 'Yeah, I got to get goods and bow.'

Lang raised his eyebrows.

'Then come on in here so I get tend them wounds of yours, boy,' he said with a curl of his finger. 'You need stitching up real bad before you end up like that damn lumberjack.'

Iron Eyes was about to do as he was told when another thought came to him. He walked back to Smith's body and plucked the gun off the boards, tucked it into his pants and then stepped down on to the street sand and retrieved the unconscious Barker's six-shooter as well. He stepped up on to the boardwalk and trailed the smaller man into the store.

Lang could not see what the blood-covered youngster was holding in his skeletal hands as he entered the general store and moved to where Lang was standing.

'What you got there, boy?' Lang asked without turning around as he made his way to the long counter.

The slender youth gave out a muted laugh.

'Guns, Kerm,' Iron Eyes said excitedly. 'I got guns.'

TEN

It was more than an hour later when Bo Hartson looked up at the mysterious Iron Eyes as the tall youngster rounded the corner and entered the livery. Hartson barely recognized the youngster decked out in brand new shirt and pants as he walked back toward where the blacksmith was seated.

Iron Eyes was labouring under the weight of carrying his boxed goods. Every hidden graze hurt as the cardboard box rubbed against the simple clothing Lang had given him. The burly blacksmith got to his feet and looked at the bruised and battered Iron Eyes as he strolled toward the forge and then carefully laid down a cardboard box next to his muscular pal.

'Iron Eyes got whiskey and cigars.' The youngster beamed as he pointed at the box. 'We smoke and drink now.'

The blacksmith stroked his whiskered chin and stared at the clothes his protégé now sported.

'How'd you get these new duds, boy?' he asked.

'Kerm give me,' Iron Eyes answered. 'He find lot of dollars on dead man.'

Hartson raised his eyebrows. 'Exactly what dead man would that be, son?'

Iron Eyes looked at his curious friend.

'The man I killed in fight, Bo,' he shrugged as he inspected his goods in the box like a child staring into a jar full of candy canes. 'He not need money. Him dead.'

The blacksmith exhaled and plucked two tin cups off the side of his forge and placed them on one of the upturned barrels he used as seats. He then moved closer to Iron Eyes and cautiously asked.

'Was that anything to do with the shooting I heard?' he asked his young pal as he silently noticed the cuts and bruises that covered his gaunt features.

Iron Eyes nodded.

'Two big men start shooting at Iron Eyes,' he explained with a casual shrug. 'I made one sleep but the other kept trying to shoot me with gun. I killed him with knife.'

Hartson gave a big sigh and rubbed his neck. He walked around the lean figure and then looked down into the box at the goods within it.

'Looks like you got a good deal with old Kermit, boy,' he noted. 'You did darn well for yourself.'

'Kerm is good man,' Iron Eyes agreed before reaching down and lifting the cigar box up. He opened its lid and offered one of the black cigars to the blacksmith. 'We smoke now.'

'You bought most of his store by the looks of you, Iron Eyes,' Hartson said as he picked one of the cigars as sniffed it carefully. 'Why'd Kermit give you these clothes, boy? Your other clothes looked OK.'

'Clothes bloody,' Iron Eyes said. 'Ripped by fatman and his bullets. Kerm said these better.'

The blacksmith nodded as he visually inspected Iron Eyes' new wardrobe. He rubbed his chin.

'They are kinda smart,' Hartson said. 'Darn fancy.'

'Will snare many furs for Kerm,' Iron Eyes said.

The blacksmith placed the cigar in his mouth, leaned over the forge and lit the long thin smoke. He puffed and then returned his attention to his youthful friend. His eyes could see the gun grips poking out of Iron Eyes' belt as he rested his bulk on to the small upturned barrel.

'Where you get the guns, boy?' he asked as smoke drifted from his mouth. 'Did Kermit sell them to you?'

Iron Eyes shook his head and helped himself to one of his cigars before placing the box back down next to the whiskey bottles.

'They logger's guns,' he stated. 'I take.'

'Is that so?' Hartson muttered.

'I take guns from them,' Iron Eyes continued.

The blacksmith raised his bushy eyebrows. 'Did you?'

'Now they mine, Bo,' the thin man copied Hartson's actions by the forge and used the hot coals to ignite his own cigar. 'One man was asleep and the other did not have any more use for his gun. Him dead.'

Hartson pulled the cigar from his mouth and blew a line of smoke at the dirt floor. He had spent his entire life studying every known brand of man but he could not fathom Iron Eyes. He sat back down and leaned forward.

'You said they shot at you?' he asked.

'Them bad men. Bad fight,' Iron Eyes said as he filled his lungs with the strong smoke and then lifted his shirt to display his savage wounds. 'Look what they did. Skin ripped open.'

Hartson bit his lip as he stared at the hideous grazes.

'You in pain, boy?' he asked.

Iron Eyes nodded. 'Hurt bad.'

'I figured you were involved when we heard the shooting start up,' the blacksmith inhaled more smoke and then allowed it to drift between his teeth. 'Looks like old Kermit got his needle and thread out and darned you up like a pair of socks.'

'Kerm did good job,' Iron Eyes said through gritted teeth. 'Men started fighting Iron Eyes. We fight hard. I had to kill one to stop him.'

Hartson sighed and then returned the cigar to his mouth as he watched the young hunter staring into the flickering flames that danced between the coals. He then looked at the huge barn doors and noticed that the sun was going down. The bright sunlight had been replaced by mysterious twilight.

'It's getting dark,' he said glancing at the tall man as he puffed on his cigar. 'It'll be pitch black before you get back to the forest.'

Iron Eyes gave a nod of his head. 'Good. It better when it dark. Enemies cannot see you so easy in dark.'

'Yep,' Hartson inhaled deeply as his friend's words sank into his tired mind. He knew that Silver Creek was overflowing with men who might decide to seek revenge for what the naïve youngster had done to one of their breed. It made him nervous but Iron Eyes appeared oblivious to any possible threat. 'Them lumberjacks might have themselves a few friends that will try to make you pay for winning that fight, Iron Eyes.'

The gaunt hunter stared through his cigar smoke at the blacksmith. He was confused by the words Hartson had just uttered.

'What do you mean?'

Hartson rested his hands on his knees.

'They might figure on teaching you a lesson, son,' he said. 'They might try to finish what them two lumberjacks started. They might try to kill you themselves.'

Iron Eyes still did not understand his pal's concerns.

'Why?' he asked. 'Fight over.'

The blacksmith looked at the naïve expression on the face of the younger man. Iron Eyes knew little of the real world, Hartson thought. He knew only the forest and the Indians and creatures that roamed within its confines. There was probably no concept there of vengeance. The lumberjacks were a different breed to those that Iron Eyes was used to. They held a grudge and that could come back to haunt the emaciated young hunter.

'You made them loggers look pitiful, boy,' Hartson explained. 'You whipped them and men like them don't take kindly to being made to look pitiful.'

'I no savvy,' Iron Eyes shrugged as his teeth gripped the cigar. 'They not scare me. I not run away. I only fight when I have to fight.'

The blacksmith decided to change the subject. He glanced at the gun grips poking from the pants belt of the youngster and pointed at them.

'You know how to use them guns, boy?' he asked.

'I will learn,' Iron Eyes said confidently.

Hartson smiled. 'I'm damn sure that you will.'

Iron Eyes looked around the livery and then pulled the cigar from his mouth. 'Where are men that give you your winnings, Bo?'

The blacksmith grinned.

'Luke and Charlie got liquored up after you left,' he explained. 'They staggered off to sleep it off.'

The naïve young hunter still had difficulty understanding the complicated language he had only recently begun to learn. He stared blankly at his burly companion.

'Sleep what off?' Iron Eyes wondered.

'They were drunk, Iron Eyes,' Hartson joked. 'They polished off my bottle between them in record time.'

Iron Eyes thought that everyone had the same constitution as himself. He could not comprehend what the blacksmith meant by saying the old loggers were drunk.

'What does drunk mean?' he pressed.

The blacksmith knew that it was pointless continuing. He stood and patted the wide bony shoulder of his young pal and grinned.

'They were just tuckered out,' he grinned.

The blacksmith walked slowly to the massive barn doors and glanced out at the crowded street. Even though a score or more blazing torches now illuminated the town as darkness crept across the rolling hills, the drunken festivities were far from over. Hartson paused and looked at Iron Eyes who was standing behind his muscular shoulder.

'What is going on, Bo?' Iron Eyes wondered as he too noticed men flooding out from various buildings and gathering again. 'Are they having another fight?'

'Nope,' Hartson said through a cloud of smoke. 'They're gonna have themselves a horse race.'

'Horse race?' Iron Eyes considered the words. 'Men bet dollars again?'

'Yep, that's what they're gonna do,' the blacksmith agreed. 'They always have themselves a horse race to round off the day.'

Hartson sucked in cigar smoke as his eyes focused

on a half dozen horses and riders being gathered at the far end of town. He removed the cigar from his lips and pointed it at the horses.

'They're gonna race them horses, boy,' the larger man noted. 'The gamblers always arrange a horse race when the prize fight ends early.'

'Men bet dollars again?' Iron Eyes repeated.

'Yep, they'll be betting big money,' Hartson chuckled.

'White men are loco,' Iron Eyes spat in disgust. 'They play games like little people.'

'You mean kids?' the blacksmith questioned.

Iron Eyes squinted hard at the totally odd sight of riders and horses getting ready to race and grunted his disapproval at the sight. The crowd were exchanging banknotes and other valuable items in a fevered fashion in readiness of the impending race.

Then the darkness at the far end of Silver Creek lit up for a fraction of a second as someone fired a starting gun. The ear-splitting sound of the gun was only matched by the excited howls and cheers of the gathered audience.

Iron Eyes flinched in surprise as the gunshot rang out. Both he and Hartson watched as the half dozen horsemen spurred and started racing. They could feel the ground beneath their feet start to tremble as pounding hoofs raced down the street toward them.

The hunter placed a hand on the muscular shoulder of the blacksmith and watched in awe as the six horsemen galloped past the livery stable.

Both he and Hartson screwed up their eyes as dust filled the eerie torchlight. Silver Creek rocked as hundreds of men cheered. The six riders continued to spur their mounts as they headed toward the outskirts of town. The cloud of choking dust which followed in the wake of the horses hung in the early evening air and mocked all attempts for the onlookers to observe the riders.

'There they go, boy,' Hartson exhaled and clapped his monstrous hands. 'They'll head on around the town until they reach the old windmill and then come on back.'

Iron Eyes had no interest in the race itself but he was interested in the horses. He frowned and pushed his limp mane off his face and began to think.

The blacksmith turned and looked up into Iron Eyes' thoughtful face. He could tell that the youngster had suddenly had a notion.

'What you thinking about, boy?' he pressed.

'I was thinking that I should have a horse,' he muttered aloud. 'A horse could take me to places.'

'You ain't got enough money to buy any of the nags in my stable let alone a good one,' Hartson said bluntly. 'Horses are valuable in these parts.'

Iron Eyes considered the blacksmith's words.

'Did the man I kill have a horse, Bo?' Iron Eyes asked as he traced a thumbnail along his jaw. 'If he did, I take his horse.'

The blacksmith shook his head at his companion's idea.

95

'Listen up, you can't go taking a man's horse, Iron Eyes,' Hartson said firmly as he followed Iron Eyes back into the heart of the livery. 'They lynch folks that steal horses around here.'

Iron Eyes was confused. He hesitated and looked back at Hartson.

'But man is dead,' Iron Eyes frowned. 'He not need a horse now. His horse is mine. That is the law of the forest.'

Hartson marched after Iron Eyes, rested a hand on the shoulder of the young man and turned him.

'Listen, boy,' he pressed. 'This ain't the forest. If you take even a dead man's horse, they'll kill you for sure. If you want a horse you'll have to buy one.'

Again Iron Eyes considered his idea of how to get his hands on a horse. Then a wry smile etched his face.

'Or steal one,' Iron Eyes grinned as his bony fingers pushed his long limp hair off his face.

'You can't do that, Iron Eyes,' Hartson argued. 'They'll hang you for sure if you do.'

'Not white men's horses,' the gaunt hunter smiled.

The large liveryman glared into the bullet-coloured eyes of his tall friend and shook his head. 'What you got cooking in that conniving head of yours, boy?'

Iron Eyes curled his finger as he had seen Kermit Lang do an hour before. The blacksmith moved closer.

'Injuns have many ponies,' he said drily as he

lifted one of the whiskey bottles from the box. 'I have seen them around their camp.'

The blacksmith rubbed his mouth on the back of his sleeve as he watched Iron Eyes extract the bottle's cork with his sharp teeth and spit it at the forge.

'Are you figuring stealing an Injun pony?' he gasped.

Iron Eyes filled the tin cups and handed one to his friend. As the large man accepted the cup he watched Iron Eyes staring into the hard liquor.

'Injuns not hang people,' the hunter grinned. 'Not like white men.'

The blacksmith downed the powerful whiskey in one swallow and held his tin cup out for a refill. As Iron Eyes poured more of the amber liquor into his cup, Hartson sighed.

'Reckon them Injuns ain't as savage as civilized folks tend to be when it comes to horse flesh, boy.'

Iron Eyes took a sip of whiskey and nodded in agreement.

ELEVEN

The sky had darkened since the dishevelled Iron Eyes had left the pair of lumberjacks lying in pools of their own blood outside the general store. Only the bright moon gave any hint of the strange hunter as he silently approached the vast forest with his box of goods in his bony hands. With every stride he sensed that he was being observed from the depths of the woodland and yet he did not slow his pace. Iron Eyes wanted to dissolve into the land he knew so well. Few if any of the forest's many creatures could disappear quite as effortlessly as the tall youngster, but he had many years of practice behind him.

Iron Eyes paused for a moment and stood like a stone statue in the long swaying grass. The moon was making everything appear to be painted in a deathly shade of blue.

His eyes darted in their sockets at the wall of trees that faced him. Every inch of his honed instincts told him that someone or something was watching his approach. A bead of sweat rolled down from his hair and navigated a route over his bony face until it finally dropped from his chin.

He was only too aware that he had left himself vulnerable by leaving the protective cover of the forest hours earlier and was now probably being observed as he returned.

Iron Eyes rested the cardboard box down on a tree stump and adjusted the bow still residing on his shoulder. The grips of the two deadly .45s poked out from his pants as his long digits fished out one of his cigars from his shirt pocket. He then produced one of the matches Kermit Lang had given him and scratched it across a gun grip.

The match erupted in his cupped hands as he raised it to the end of his cigar. He sucked the strong smoke deep into his lungs and stared ahead through the flickering flame. For a fleeting moment his bruised features were caught in the faltering light. He then shook the match and tossed its twisted black length aside as his eyes still searched for any hint of the eyes he was convinced were watching him.

Iron Eyes pulled the cigar from his mouth and allowed the smoke to filter from between his teeth. He then returned the long weed to his mouth and snorted like a caged mountain lion in readiness.

The fearless youth filled his lungs again with smoke and then stroked the grips of his six-shooters. He knew that none of the Indians had the range to reach him with their arrows from the forest. A wry grin etched his face as he picked up the box and held it to his belly. He walked to where the grass was highest and then vanished from view as he continued on toward the trees.

The vast forest was deathly quiet as Iron Eyes moved back into its confines. The gaunt hunter used every shadow, tree and dense undergrowth to his advantage as he moved unseen toward his goal. A sudden chill crept down his backbone as once again he sensed the danger which he knew was getting closer with each beat of his heart. He glanced upward at the tree canopy and then returned his icy stare at his surroundings. The large moon might have been bright outside the forest but even its rays could not fully penetrate the foliage. Only narrow wisps of moonlight travelled a crooked trail down into the belly of the forest.

The tall youngster paused for a moment and listened hard to his surroundings. Experience told Iron Eyes that something was wrong.

Something was very wrong.

Even if he could not actually see them, he knew they were close. Whether it was animals or Indians, he sensed that they had to be moving in his direction.

He spat the cigar at the damp ground and crushed it underfoot as his eyes flashed in the eerie illumination of the forest gloom. The scent of the cigar was alien to the dense woodland but Iron Eyes did not care, for he had other things burning into his mind.

He realized that he had to reach one of his many dens and hide his goods before he could venture deeper into the forest and find answers to his countless questions. Iron Eyes knew every sound in the forest yet no matter how hard he strained to hear, there was nothing. Not one solitary sound.

Like the wolves which had raised him, he sniffed the cold night air. His eyes and ears might not be able to detect anything, but his keen sense of smell did.

There was a faint scent on the soft breeze which moved through the forest. It was the familiar aroma of burning. The Indians had a campfire lit somewhere close, he told himself. His eyes narrowed and studied the tree canopies in search of reflected light that would dance against the overhead branches. After a few moments Iron Eyes caught a brief glimpse of scarlet wisps of light as they danced on the underside of the branches.

He strode up an embankment and paused.

Something was wrong though.

The Indians had lit a campfire far closer than usual.

His honed instincts were tingling. Every hair on the nape of his neck had risen to alert him. Iron Eyes moved through the undergrowth swiftly until he found one of the many places he used to keep out of sight from his many enemies. Ever since he had been a small child Iron Eyes had learned from the timber wolves to make scores of small dens so that his enemies could never know where he was.

The youngster stooped under seemingly impenetrable undergrowth and carefully slid down a slope to the base of a massive oak. He brushed the sharp brambles aside and found what he had been seeking.

A hollowed out section beneath the tree suddenly presented itself to Iron Eyes. He pushed the box containing his cigars and whiskey bottles into the dark interior and then pushed the grass and sharp brambles across the secret den.

Iron Eyes then straightened up. He looked all about him once more and gritted his teeth as he made his way under another mass of dense brush and climbed back up the slope.

The forest was still quiet.

Iron Eyes had never known it so quiet.

Even the animals made no noise. They too sensed the approaching danger, he reasoned. Silently the gaunt figure raced up a slippery slope to the top of a tree-covered hill and crouched in the shadows of the elms and oaks.

He sniffed at the forest air again. This time he was certain that a number of Indians were carefully making their way toward the very spot where he rested on one knee. In all his days, he had never known a hunting party to venture to this part of the forest.

Why were they doing so now? He silently wondered.

For what felt like an eternity, the young hunter

tried to make sense of the fact that the Indians were hunting in a place that they knew had very little game. The only things which shared this part of the forest with Iron Eyes were bears and mountain lions. Neither of which were good eating.

The young hunters might be after furs, he reasoned, but even that seemed doubtful. Bears provided good furs for their lodges, but were far more easily hunted down and killed during the winter months when they took their long sleeps.

Iron Eyes could not make any sense from his mortal enemies hunting in this part of the dense forest. There was little game to be had here. Indians were not satisfied with mere rabbits as he was. They needed something to feed the entire tribe.

Something like elk or moose.

So why were the Indians moving through this section of the forest? The question gnawed at his craw until the obvious answer suddenly dawned on Iron Eyes.

They were hunting him.

They had to be, Iron Eyes thought. They did not want something to eat, they wanted something to kill.

TWELVE

With the sudden realization that he was no longer the hunter but the hunted, Iron Eyes felt uneasy as he moved through the shadows from tree to tree. His eyes darted from one part of the forest to another in a vain search for the Indians that his flared nostrils sensed. Apart from countless trees of every type and size, he saw nothing in the eerie twilight.

Iron Eyes rose to his full height and rested against a stout broad leaf tree. He sniffed the air and caught the distinctive aroma of the Indians again.

All creatures have their own distinctive scent and Iron Eyes knew them all. His flared nostrils were so skilled at locating the various creatures within the confines of the vast forest, he could even tell how many individual creatures he was honed on to. There were roughly six Indians moving silently toward him, he told himself.

Iron Eyes bit his lower lip as his mind raced.

He had tackled more than six warriors before, but it was never easy. His bony hands gripped the bow which hung over his left shoulder and checked the arrow-filled quiver.

The gaunt hunter knew exactly why the Indians were moving through the dense undergrowth in his direction. For years he had used his superior agility to steal whatever he wanted from the Indians' encampments. He had relieved them of the bow and the arrows only a week earlier.

He had also made off with a leg of venison as well during the same raid. The Indians had obviously decided to put an end to the man they knew as Ayan-Ees, the evil one.

Every year or so the tribe's young Indians would take it upon themselves to attempt to capture and kill the elusive Iron Eyes, who was a thorn in their collective sides. Their failures had only added to the stories of the ghost who would not die.

Most men would have shied away from potentially deadly trouble, but Iron Eyes was unlike most men. He had no fear of anyone or anything. Death was something he knew was inevitable so he faced it head on.

Every creature within the forest had gone to ground, he thought. All except the Indians, who he knew were getting closer and closer.

Unlike Iron Eyes, the Indians could not move silently through the vast forest like a fleeting shadow.

When he hunted, none of his chosen prey had any notion that death was on the prowl.

Iron Eyes placed his ear against the hollow trunk of the tree next to him and listened. The moccasin-covered feet of the advancing Indians made sounds that were magnified by the hollow trunk of the tree.

His eyes flashed around the untamed terrain until he worked out exactly where they were. A mass of dense darkness stood between the young hunter and the Indians who were heading in his direction.

Entangled ivy and razor-sharp brambles covered the slope and held the tree trunks together like netting. Iron Eyes knew that the Indians were just beyond the impenetrable undergrowth.

The dark interior of the forest was protecting the tall misfit from a direct attack. He screwed up his eyes and began to wonder why his mortal enemies were venturing into this section of the woodland.

It seemed strange to the hunter that the Indians were this far east of their camp. They tended to hunt and trap on the other side of the forest where the game was more varied and abundant.

Why were they in this part of the forest?

The question taunted Iron Eyes. With the cunning the timber wolves had imparted to him years before, he stooped and moved swiftly along the tree-covered ridge.

When he stopped, Iron Eyes knew that he had encircled the hunting warriors. But even his keen

106

eyes could still not see them in the half light.

The massive trees were in full leaf. Everything beneath the top of the high branches was starved of light. Only slender shafts of moonlight managed to filter through the darkness and find the floor of the woods.

Iron Eyes looked upward.

He knew that if he were going to be able to see the Indians clearly he would have to get above them. Most men of Iron Eyes' height would be far too heavy to climb up the trees, but not the emaciated hunter.

A lifetime of starvation had taken its toll on his tall wiry frame. Iron Eyes was far leaner than most but had learned how to use this to his advantage. His long thin arm stretched out and grabbed a sturdy branch. His bony fingers got a firm grip of the slippery wood and hauled the rest of his emaciated body off the ground.

Within seconds he had ascended the lofty tree until he was roughly thirty feet off the ground. Had he been heavier the branches might have snapped but Iron Eyes was able to rest upon a branch without it even bending. Iron Eyes was so light that he was able to travel from one tree to another without fear of branches breaking under his boots.

After negotiating his way across the heavily leafed branches and using every shadow to his advantage, Iron Eyes finally spotted them.

Six warriors armed with bows moved stealthily

through the undergrowth below his high vantage point. Iron Eyes narrowed his eyes and focused down on them.

They were a hunting party, he thought.

But they were not hunting game.

They were after the one creature within the dense forest that had always eluded them. He crouched down and balanced on a wide branch.

Iron Eyes knew that they were hunting him. For years the young Indians had tried to earn the respect of their elders by trying to capture or kill the elusive Ayan-Ees.

They wanted his mane of long black hair as a trophy.

For they were all too aware that the warrior who achieved this feat and defeated the living ghost would become a legend amongst his fellow Indians and be proclaimed their chief.

It sounded a lot easier than it actually was, for Iron Eyes knew the forest far better than any of them. He had travelled every inch of the vast tree-covered terrain during the days when he hunted with the pack of timber wolves.

Balancing on a branch like an expert tightrope walker, Iron Eyes removed his own bow from his shoulder and then primed its taut string with one of his arrows. He closed one eye and then stared down at the six men below his high parapet and watched them.

Their faces were covered in paint that, even from

his lofty perch far above them, Iron Eyes could see. It was obvious to the young bowman that his instincts had been definitely right.

They were hunting him.

THIRTEEN

There was no hesitation in Iron Eyes as he released the arrow down upon his feathered adversaries. The lethal projectile hummed in the eerily cold air as it flew down from the high branch. One of the young Indians arched as the arrow buried itself into his neck and fell at the feet of his fellow searchers.

Yet even before the arrow had found its target, Iron Eyes had moved from the high branch that he had been balanced upon and disappeared into the overhanging foliage. As the startled Indian warriors swung around in search of the archer, Iron Eyes had primed his bow again and fired another arrow at them.

Hysterical chants filled the depths of the darkness as his second arrow landed between them. Within seconds the remaining warriors had started firing up into the trees.

Iron Eyes remained unseen against the trunk of a tree as arrows tore through the overhanging leaves and peppered the branch in futile response.

A wry grin carved a route across his youthful face as Iron Eyes swiftly placed another of his deadly arrows on his bow, drew back on its string and fired down at the startled Indians.

Once again Iron Eyes moved from where he had fired and leapt like a mountain lion from behind the tree trunk to another branch. As the branch rocked under him he heard the Indians arrows tearing through the shadowy canopy.

He gritted his teeth, lay across the branch and pushed some of the entangled branches aside until he was able to see the frantic Indians loading their bows again.

Iron Eyes screwed up his eyes and looked down at his handiwork. One of the warriors lay dead and another was howling in agony as he tried to pull an arrow from his fleshy thigh.

A satisfied smile crossed his face as he placed another arrow on his bowstring. He drew back on the taut string and fired down at the four remaining Indians who were still trying to work out where the elusive Iron Eyes was.

One of the Indians was knocked off his feet as the arrow went through his chest guard into his flesh. Iron Eyes could not tell whether the arrow had killed or just maimed its target, but that did not matter to the lean hunter.

He athletically got to his feet, raced along the branch and then jumped from one tree to another.

Every leaf-laden branch shook as Iron Eyes hit the tree hard. His hands desperately grabbed at the slender trunk as his feet slipped on the damp branches. For a brief heart-stopping moment the gaunt youngster thought that he was going to fall until his hands finally got a firm hold on the tree.

As he steadied himself against the slender tree trunk, Iron Eyes realized that the bow snapped as he had collided with the tree. Angrily he cast the broken weapon aside. The bow did not fall far as its string got snagged on a branch just below the one he was standing upon.

A cruel look manifested on his haunting features as he gazed down at the remaining warriors far below him. A hundred thoughts flashed through his mind as his boots searched for a firm footing.

Arrows ripped through the leafy canopy all around his lean body. Broken twigs and leaves showed over Iron Eyes as his foes still tried to kill the man they considered to be almost immortal.

'I hate Injuns,' he hissed through his gritted teeth before he clambered down to a lower broader branch. He rested a hand on the tree trunk and licked his dry lips.

Then he remembered the guns pushed down into his pants belt. Their cold steel pressed against his belly as his fertile mind began to hatch another plan.

Iron Eyes drew one of the weapons and stared at it, bathed in the shimmering moonlight. He knew of the destruction the gun could unleash but was fearful of firing it. He recalled the words that Kermit Lang had uttered when he had just confiscated the weapons from the lumberjacks.

He did not know how to use these six-shooters.

Iron Eyes was also well aware of the fact that when you pulled on their triggers a blinding flash would spew from the barrel. That as well as the deafening noise made him nervously unwilling to fire such weapons.

Then another thought came to the gaunt hunter.

If he were to leave the forest and venture out into the land where the white men dominated, he needed to become an expert with guns.

Cautiously his thumb pulled back on the gun hammer until it locked into position. He had watched Drew Smith doing this during their fateful encounter.

His heart was pounding furiously inside his bony chest as he aimed the gun through the branches at the Indians. The gun was far heavier than Iron Eyes had imagined and his hand began to shake.

He pulled back on the trigger hard.

The explosion rocked the lean hunter. The bullet cut through the trees like a hot knife through butter and hit the ground between the warriors.

To the utter surprise of Iron Eyes, the Indians gathered up their wounded and started to flee the area. The sound of the gun had frightened the braves as they had no experience of six-guns, just like Iron Eyes when he had first entered Silver Creek.

113

Iron Eyes had never seen anyone so frightened before and it both amused and troubled him. The Indians were long gone as the lean figure descended from the tree and crouched on the ground beside the towering tree.

Smoke billowed from the barrel of the six-shooter as he slowly straightened up to his full height and gazed to where he had witnessed the warriors retreating.

He looked at the gun in his hand in a mixture of surprise and awe. He had never seen the Indians move quite so fast before and knew that it had nothing to do with him. It had been the unexpected fury which the six-gun had unleashed at them.

Iron Eyes moved silently across the uneven ground toward the body of the Indian he had killed with his arrow and studied it.

There was no emotion in his gaunt features as he pushed the gun back into his pants belt next to its companion. He then glanced over his shoulder to where the Indians had fled only moments before.

He removed the Indian's bow to replace his own and hung it over his arm. The tall figure pushed his bony fingers through his long hair as his eyes narrowed.

'Now me hunt them,' he whispered before smiling. 'And get horse.'

FOURTEEN

The forest began to reflect the sound of the gentle night breeze which swept through the trees yet Iron Eyes did not hear anything except the frightened hearts of the men he was tracking. Like a determined bloodhound on the scent of an elusive racoon, the young hunter followed the Indians for more than three miles through the rugged terrain. The deeper he got into the vast interior the stronger the scent of the main tribe became. He sniffed at the night air and detected the aromatic smell of cooking.

Saliva dripped from the corners of his mouth as he forged on in pursuit of his prey, yet Iron Eyes had no intention of catching the fleeing Indians. All he wanted to do was find their new camp and steal one of their ponies.

With the honed and ruthless determination which he had learned from the timber wolves years before, Iron Eyes continued to track the terrified warriors through the dense undergrowth. Nothing could slow his progress as he used every shadow to his advantage.

Brief wisps of moonlight betrayed the Indians ahead of him as his determined eyes watched them carrying their wounded comrades. He knew that he could kill them at any moment but that was not his way.

There was no profit in killing Indians.

It was a total waste of his time and energy. Iron Eyes had only killed one of the hunting party because he knew from bitter experience what would have happened to him if he had not done anything.

But the youngster still hated being forced to defend himself against an enemy who he knew would never be satisfied with anything other than his own demise.

Silently, Iron Eyes travelled deeper into the depths of the woodland. Even though he knew that he could skilfully pick each of them off with well-placed arrows, he had no desire to do so. All he wanted to do was frighten them away from his own many secret lairs.

As his bullet-coloured eyes focused on the fleeing men ahead of him, he gave out a bone-chilling howl and then sent an arrow over their heads. The warriors hastened their pace.

'Injuns not come back soon,' he whispered as he glanced up at the tree tops. A thought flashed through his mind as he returned the bow to his shoulder.

116

They were utterly defeated as far as he was concerned.

Iron Eyes would leave them be if they continued to run away, he thought. Then he glanced back up at the tree tops above him. There was a more pressing notion burning in his fevered mind. One which he had momentarily forgotten during his brief but bloody encounter with the hunting party.

'Must get horse,' he muttered.

He knew that there was only one way he could get his hands on horseflesh and that was to steal one. The Indians had many ponies and, unlike the white lumberjacks in Silver Creek, they had no laws to say that he could not do just that.

As he continued to move forward, Iron Eyes reasoned that stealing an Indian pony was no different than stealing anything else from them. He had always braved their fury to get anything he wanted. The bow and its arrows, which hung from his wide shoulder, had been obtained that way. Even the long-bladed knife in his boot had been stolen one dark night from under the nose of a sleeping Indian.

In his naïve mind, there was no difference in stealing anything he desired from the Indians. Even a fully-grown pony was fair game in his mind.

Iron Eyes paused and looked upward again. He knew that if he were to reach the Indian camp before the warriors did, he could do so far faster by using the high branches.

Iron Eyes located one of his precious cigars in the

117

breast pocket of his shirt and placed its twisted length in the corner of his mouth as his mind wandered.

Until he had witnessed the riders in Silver Creek, a few hours earlier, Iron Eyes had never even given a second thought to horseflesh. Yet the mere sight of the horsemen as they raced around the remote town had fuelled his imagination.

Horses were the means to escape this land.

Iron Eyes had instantly known that he had to get one.

The tall hunter struck a match and raised its flickering flame to the cigar. He sucked hard and filled his lungs with smoke as he pondered on the thought of having a horse of his own. The cupped flame of the match was extinguished as he exhaled the line of smoke at it.

Suddenly it was virtually pitch black once again.

His narrowed eyes adjusted swiftly to the darkness that shrouded his pitifully lean form. After nearly two decades, his eyes were used to the eerie twilight. Even though there was no moonlight capable of penetrating the dark hollow in which Iron Eyes found himself in, he could still see the warriors carrying their wounded back to their new camp.

The camp was far closer than he had originally thought.

As his bony fingers pulled the cigar from his lips, he sniffed the cold forest air and began nodding to himself. His flared nostrils could smell the signs of their camp. They were far stronger now, he told

118

himself.

Iron Eyes could also hear the faint vocals of untold numbers of Indians in the encampment. He inhaled the cigar again and returned his attention to the black cobweb of interlocking branches above him.

He focused hard.

Strange light reflected off the high canopy.

The Indian camp was no more than a half mile away, he calculated. He filled his lungs again and then cast the cigar aside. He rubbed his hands together in anticipation of the climb.

Soon he would find their ponies, he told himself.

With an agility normally rationed to the forest's mountain lions, Iron Eyes hastily ascended the tree. He kept climbing until reached the vast expanse of thick foliage and then started to move from tree to tree. There was no fear in the youngster as he leapt from one branch to another, even though at times he was at least sixty feet above the forest floor.

With each leap, Iron Eyes drew closer to his ultimate goal, the newly established Indian camp. The light from their numerous campfires began dancing against the tree trunks far beneath the fearless young hunter. He did not slow his progress toward the isolated camp and after only a few strenuous leaps, he started to be able to make out movement, signs of life far below him.

Like the phantom that many of the forest people considered him to be, Iron Eyes had no equal when it came to tracking anyone or anything. His unequalled skills were more akin to that of an animal than a man for he used every one of his senses in the manner most wild creatures do.

Iron Eyes had perfected his unrivalled abilities by watching and learning from the animals that filled the forest. As a child he had quickly perfected the way that wolves hunted at ground level and then noticed the way squirrels and chipmunks moved through the trees.

There was nothing that Iron Eyes could not track or kill and that included those which attempted to end his life as well.

Even the mighty grizzly bear had proven no match for the tempestuous Iron Eyes when the young hunter had been cornered by the great beast. Some have said that there is nothing more dangerous than a cornered or wounded animal.

Iron Eyes was equally as dangerous as any of the forest's wild beasts. He still retained the merciless ways of the ferocious timber wolves that had raised him, as well as the wisdom of the animals that had always eluded his traps.

Unlike the men he had encountered at Silver Creek, Iron Eyes knew nothing of revenge or any of their even worse habitual traits. When he killed it was because he had to kill in order to survive.

There was never any hatred burning in his guts.

In the harsh terrain of the unforgiving forest, you either survived or you died. There was no other alternative.

Life and death were exactly the same to the pitifully thin hunter as he moved silently through the
tree canopies ever closer to the Indian encampment.
He knew that if he were to make just one mistake, he
would die.

His eyes gazed down into the middle of the camp
as he approached through the heavily leafed tree
tops. Fires burned intently as numerous fragrant
meals were being readied by the females.

Iron Eyes had never seen so many of the Indians
before.

There were far more of them milling around in
the unmarked boundaries of the camp than he had
ever imagined. As the gaunt figure came to rest
beside a high tree trunk he stared down upon them
curiously. Then he remembered that every one of
previous visits had all taken place after most of the
tribe were asleep inside the tepees. He rubbed the
sweat from his hollow features and pushed his long
black hair back. He crouched on a branch and rested
his backbone against the trunk of the tree.

'Many braves,' he whispered. 'Many she-braves
too.'

FIFTEEN

Every saloon or meeting place in Silver Ccreek resounded to the raised voices of angry men as the story of what had happened to Drew Smith and the more fortunate Hog Barker. None of the muscular tree fellers gave a second thought to the fact that what the bruised and bloodied Barker was saying meant that the emaciated stranger known as Iron Eyes had been forced to fight for his very life. All the drunken crowd was concerned about was the fact that one of their own was dead.

Hog Barker had embroidered a good if totally inaccurate version of what had actually happened in the main street. There was no mention of the fact that he and his drinking pals had gone out of their way to start a fight with what they had considered an easy target.

Barker embellished the few details he could actually remember into a story he knew would stir up the avenging venom of his whiskey-sodden fellow loggers.

It had started out with a handful of lumberjacks but as they moved from one saloon to another, the crowd had developed into practically every one of the muscular loggers.

Barker might have lost his fight with Iron Eyes but, like all men who bullied the less able, he was determined to see the youngster hanged for killing Smith.

The gangly youth was going to pay a high price, if Barker had anything to say about it. He pounded the bar counters in every saloon they trawled until even he started to believe his fictional account of what had happened during the afternoon.

'That critter gotta hang for killing Drew,' Barker screamed at the top of his voice to the dozens of lumberjacks as they supplied him with plenty of free liquor. 'He done killed like a rabid animal, boys. Me, Drew and Shake was minding our own business when this tall critter come marching down the street and attacked us.'

'Who was he?' one of the other lumberjacks asked.

'Hog already said that he was a stranger,' another of the burly men chipped in as they crowded around Barker.

Barker lowered his whiskey glass from his lips.

'He didn't look like regular folks, boys,' he drawled as he nursed his bruised face with his free hand. 'He looked like the Devil himself.'

The collective response amongst the gathering

could be heard out in the street as the blacksmith approached to find out what was happening in Silver Creek. Bo Hartson had figured that the killing of Drew Smith would not have gone down well with the majority of the townsfolk. He had been right. He rested a hand on the swing doors and gazed into the noisy interior and began shaking his head.

Hog Barker repeated his statement and then embellished it to ensure that every one of the saloon's patrons were well and truly fired up.

'That critter ain't human, I tell you,' Barker said loudly. 'He's evil. He only came to town to kill and that's exactly what he did.'

The bartender leaned over his counter.

'Was he the tall, skinny varmint with long black hair, Hog?' he asked fearfully. 'I seen him just before I started work, over by the livery. That critter gave me the willies.'

Hog Barker stomped his sturdy boot on the boards of the saloon floor and gave a nod of his head. 'That's the critter, Joe. He looked like an Injun but he weren't no type of Injun I've ever seen before. He was way too tall. All I know is that he's plumb evil.'

'Kerm Lang reckoned his name is Iron Eyes,' another of the crowd offered. 'He said that critter lives in the forest.'

'Iron Eyes ain't a man's name,' somebody ventured. 'It sure sounds like an Injun handle.'

Every eye widened, darting to the informative logger and then back at the seated Barker. The noisy

124

crowd grew even louder as a multitude of theories began to develop.

Hartson forced his way into the saloon and began to wade through the excited crowd toward Barker. The blacksmith could hear the astounding theories being brandished back and forth as he fought his way to the trouble-making Barker.

'Nobody but stinking Injuns live in them forests, boys,' Barker snarled as he downed his whiskey and held his empty glass out for one of his fellow loggers to refill it. 'Nobody human, anyways. No normal man could survive in there with all them lions and bears and Injuns for a day.'

A mutual gasp went through the assembly of loggers as their own imaginations ran riot inside their drunken minds. They moved closer to Barker as he downed his drink, stood and then grabbed the closest whiskey bottle from someone's grasp.

'If that critter even dares to enter Silver Creek again we gotta teach him it don't pay to kill one of our kind,' Barker raged. 'We gotta string him up by the neck and let him dance until his scrawny neck snaps.'

The crowd erupted into howling cheers.

'You just can't handle being bested by a scrawny youngster,' Hartson growled at the lumberjack. 'That kid made you and your pals look like a bunch of fools and now you're trying to get him lynched.'

Barker swung on his heels and glared at the black-smith angrily. He grabbed the older man and shook him.

'You calling me a liar, Bo?' he spat.

Hartson narrowed his eyes and stared straight at Barker for a few moments and then physically pushed the logger backward. He raised a sturdy finger and pointed it straight at Barker.

'I sure am, Hog,' he snorted. 'I'm calling you a big, fat liar who got his rump kicked and he wants revenge.'

Barker steadied himself and clenched his fists.

'That critter killed Drew,' he raged. 'He stuck a knife in him and killed him for no reason. If he comes back to town he's gonna kill someone else.'

'As I hear it, you and Drew picked on the scrawny bastard and started shooting at him,' Hartson stated with a nod of his head. 'Seems to me that you got off lucky that he didn't teach you the same lesson that he taught Drew.'

'What you saying?' Barker snarled.

'I'm saying that Drew was a cold-blooded killer and he got exactly what he deserved, Hog,' Hartson retorted. 'The trouble with bullies is that they don't like it when they meet their match or their betters.'

Barker spat at the floorboards between them as the gathered crowd grew even more fevered. 'Me and the boys weren't doing nothing wrong, old man. That Iron Eyes just went loco and gutted Drew.'

Before the blacksmith had time to continue his argument, one of the lumberjacks standing behind him smashed a bottle across the back of his skull. Hartson staggered and then fell at the feet of Barker.

126

Barker looked at his fellow loggers and punched the air.

'C'mon, boys,' he shouted. 'Let's get us some guns and torches and head on up to that damn forest. If that monster puts up a fight, we'll burn him out.'

Like a troupe of circus elephants, every single one of the lumberjacks mindlessly piled out of the saloon to do just as Barker had instructed them. The drunken mob was hell-bent on getting their hands on the young hunter and stretching his neck. As the noisy crowd of lumberjacks went looking for anything they might use as fiery torches, the blacksmith lay in a pool of his own blood. Blood which seeped from the brutal gash on the back of his head.

Bo Hartson lay face down upon the sawdust-covered floor utterly oblivious to what was occurring. Yet even if he had not been unconscious it was doubtful that he could have stopped the lumberjacks.

Hog Barker had gotten exactly what he wanted.

SIXTEEN

There was something going on amid the Indians as they flocked around their newly erected tepees. Iron Eyes did not know it but they were preparing a feast to celebrate the return of the hunting party. More than a thousand men, women and children had moved their entire encampment across the forest to where it now stood. The tribal elders sat cross-legged and brooded about how they had been forced to move their entire camp as the lumberjacks had encroached into their territory.

Flames from a dozen campfires burned brightly between the tents as scores of squaws of various ages went about their nightly rituals and prepared meals. When it came to laborious duties, it was only the females who actually did anything while the menfolk watched as they shared tomahawk pipes.

The aroma of cooking filled the entire area and drifted through the surrounding trees. As Iron Eyes moved through the highest branches of the trees, the scent of cooking made even his mouth water.

The gaunt figure stopped above the camp and stared down at the numerous Indians below his high perch. Iron Eyes knew that there were far more of them than he had ever been able to calculate during all the times that he had encroached into their land. Yet as he gripped a branch in one hand and hovered above them, his mind tried to work out why they had uprooted themselves and travelled into what he deemed to be his domain.

There was no way for Iron Eyes to know that the Indians had not intentionally moved toward him, but in truth had moved away from the lumberjacks on the other side of the forest. The Indians were wise enough to realize that soon their old camp would have been exposed by the felling of the woodlands most mature and valuable assets.

Iron Eyes watched them from his perilous perch curiously.

His eyes narrowed against the flickering firelight as he looked down upon them. It did not make any sense to the young hunter for an entire tribe to leave one part of the forest and go to another.

Iron Eyes knew that the hunting was far poorer here than it was at their original site. He bit his lip and then straddled the branch as he vainly tried to understand the motives behind the Indians' move.

They had not uprooted through choice, but the naïve young hunter was blissfully ignorant of this. To

his inexperienced mind, the Indians were just pro-
voking the one they considered to be an evil forest
spirit.

Iron Eyes had a simple outlook on everything.
Black or white, hunter or hunted, life or death. If
anyone wronged him, he would fight and assumed
the Indians would do the same but they were far
wiser than that. They knew that bows and arrows
were no match for the heavily-armed loggers.

Iron Eyes pondered the hundreds of people he
could see below him like a cunning cougar. The
Indians were totally unaware of his presence as
always. Just like all of the other times when he had
dared their wrath and entered their encampment,
Iron Eyes was confident that he would achieve what
he had come here to do.

He would steal one of their ponies. To him, it was
as simple as that. He did not even consider failure.
Iron Eyes smiled and then caught sight of the ponies
below his lofty perch. He squinted and stared
through the rising smoke from their many fires at the
animals hidden just beyond the dozens of tepees.

The ponies were well concealed as always, but not
from his keen eyes high above them. Iron Eyes leapt
to his feet and hurried to the very end of the stout
tree branch. With one hand holding a branch above
his head, he balanced on the slender extension.

There were at least fifteen ponies hidden from
view behind countess trees. They were far smaller
than the horseflesh Iron Eyes had seen in Silver

130

Creek but no less capable.

A crude rope encircled the sturdy animals and kept them contained between the trees. His appetite to get his hands on one of the creatures grew as he observed the animals milling around in the shadows below.

There was just one brave guarding the small herd. The Indian was seated and looked asleep to Iron Eyes. Even though he could only catch fleeting glimpses of the ponies, that was enough for the skeletal hunter.

He wanted a horse and there they were, he thought.

Iron Eyes reached down. His bony hands gripped the branch at his feet as he swung silently and then dropped to another even broader branch and steadied himself.

His mouth started to drool. Whether it was the aromatic scent of the cooking food that wafted up into the trees where he had secreted his lean form, or just being close to so many horses that had wetted his appetite, Iron Eyes was totally oblivious.

All he knew was that forty feet below his dangerously high vantage point, there were horses. He just needed one to get out of the forest.

Just one.

It had not occurred to the painfully thin young dare-devil that he had never even attempted to mount a horse, let alone ride one. In his naïve mind it could not be that difficult if white and red men alike were capable of doing it.

Iron Eyes dried his mouth on his shirt sleeve and was just about to descend from the perilously tree branch when he heard many raised voices.

He dropped on to his knees and looked through the moonlit foliage at the scene which was unfolding in the camp. The entire camp raced to where the noise was coming from as Iron Eyes silently watched.

The hunting party had returned. Other braves ran to their aid and helped support the wounded as the three young warriors fell on to their knees and accepted wooden cups of water.

With the agility of a big cat, Iron Eyes moved across the camp by the trees and then carefully climbed down to a lower branch so that he might overhear their words.

Iron Eyes remained unseen and studied the hundreds of Indians as they gathered around the three exhausted warriors who had just returned. He had learned their unique language long ago when he had first started to enter their camp to steal from them.

Iron Eyes listened intently as all three warriors embellished the story of their bloody encounter with him. A wry smile lit up his face as he slumped against the trunk of the tree.

The only truths that he heard come from any of the trio's mouths were those concerning his archery. Everything else was totally fabricated. The descriptions of Iron Eyes made it sound as if they had encountered a monster of some sort and waged a valiant battle with the creature.

To the Indians that listened intently to every word the three warriors uttered, all of the stories they had heard concerning the strange evil shadow spirit were true.

Iron Eyes frowned in utter confusion.

He knew nothing of lies or exaggeration.

SEVENTEEN

There were at least a hundred massively built lumberjacks gathered in the middle of Silver Creek as Hog Barker moved into the centre of the whiskey-soaked men. The logger had a sadistic grin on his bruised face as he pushed through the men as they lit their torches and started to wave them above their heads.

Barker clapped his hands together and then accepted a double-barrelled scattergun from Shake Norris. The evil hothead pushed two red cartridges into its chambers and then snapped it shut.

'Are you ready, boys?' he shouted above the din the mob was making. 'Are you ready to get that stinking Injun Iron Eyes and his cronies?'

The mob roared and shook their torches in answer.

'Who got the rope?' Barker asked as his eyes darted across the faces of the vengeful loggers.

'I got me a rope, Hog.' A lumberjack moved forward and patted a coiled rope, which was looped over his shoulder.

'Have y'all got guns?' Barker yelled out again.

Once again the mob growled in unison.

'Have you critters got knives?' Barker bellowed to the excited men who faced him. 'We gotta have knives so we can skin that varmint after we stretch his scrawny neck.'

The street echoed with laughter as the majority of the burly loggers echoed Barker's words. One after another knives of various sizes were drawn from the lumberjacks' belts and scabbards and raised into the night air.

The honed steel caught the bright illumination of the long torch poles wrapped in blazing coal tar. Every blade glinted in the eerily lit street as nearly every one of the lumberjacks responded to Barker's venomous ranting and displayed their knives.

Barker knew that he had achieved his goal. He had his fellow tree-fellers under his control. He continued to encourage the eager mob into hysterical chanting by shouting every vile and repugnant word in his vengeful mind.

They resembled a pack of hunting hounds with the scent of a fleeing fox in their nostrils. The crowd wanted blood. They wanted Iron Eyes' blood because that was what Barker had instilled into their drunken minds.

Silver Creek resounded to the ever-increasing

noise of the lumberjacks. The rest of the remote settlement remained off the streets for fear of falling
victim to the mob's unpredictable wrath. Barker
moved in front of his motley assembly and waved his
twin-barrelled shotgun above his head.

'C'mon, boys,' he yelled. A cruel sneer filled the
rough features of Hog Barker. He swung around on
his heels and started marching along the moonlit
street and out of Silver Creek toward the ominously
dark forest.

The intoxicated lumberjacks carried their flaming
torches above their heads and marched behind
Barker. The strange sight of the vast expanse of trees
bathed in eerie moonlight drew them like moths to
naked flames. The collective thuds of their heavy
boots seemed to shake the very ground they trod
across.

With every stride, Barker's smile grew wider.

EIGHTEEN

Like the gossamer wisps of a phantom, the athletic young hunter jumped from branch to branch unseen and unheard by anyone or anything. Iron Eyes moved through the campfire smoke above the tepees back to where he had detected the hidden ponies. As he reached a tall oak, he stopped his momentum and then dropped to the ground far below.

He landed inside the Indian camp.

Only the un-cleared brush stood between the majority of the Indians and the young hunter. Iron Eyes ran his bony fingers through his long hair and pushed it off his face. He crouched and rested the fingers of one hand on the damp soil as his other hand hovered above the knife hilt in the neck of his boot.

For what felt like an eternity, Iron Eyes just rested where he had silently landed until he was sure that none of the Indians had detected his arrival in the camp.

He squinted into the blackness and caught a satisfying brief glimpse of the horses as the small herd milled around beyond the tepees.

Slowly he rose up to his full imposing height as his narrowed eyes stared through the branches at the excited Indians two hundred yards from where he stood. None of them were concerned about anything other than their returning heroes as they flocked around the exhausted warriors.

Iron Eyes clenched his fists angrily as he recalled the words the warriors had uttered to the rest of the tribe. They had managed to make themselves sound more like heroes than what they truly were.

They were nothing but defeated, Iron Eyes thought as he watched the distant proceedings with an icy stare. Then as one of the ponies snorted, his attention returned to why he had dared enter the Indian encampment.

Iron Eyes pulled one of his recently acquired six-shooters from his belt and held its wooden grip firmly in his hand. He moved silently through the undergrowth toward the tepees between the ponies and himself. The sleeping Indian who it seemed was meant to guard the horses, had not moved an inch from where he sat.

Without pausing for even a heartbeat, Iron Eyes stepped up beside the Indian and then smashed the gun barrel across the top of the brave's scalp. As the

Indian fell on to his side, blood ran freely from the savage wound.

Iron Eyes glanced over his shoulder and then wiped the hot sticky gore from the gun on to his shirt tail. He pushed the gun back into his pants next to the other and then carefully stepped over the body.

His skeletal hand pushed the branches apart, allowing a narrow gap for him to slide his slender frame through. He had only just entered the enclosure where the ponies were gathered when he heard an unfamiliar noise coming from over his left shoulder.

The tall gaunt figure twisted on his heels and stared vainly into the shadows. His eyes searched the dark corner of the roped-off section of the enclosure for what had made the strange sound which had alerted his honed senses.

Iron Eyes was bewildered by the noise he was listening to.

It was unlike anything he had ever heard before and it troubled the tall hunter. Without making a single sound, Iron Eyes stooped, pulled the long knife from the neck of his boot and then straightened back up.

He gripped the handle of the long-bladed dagger and aimed its lethally sharp point to where he could hear the strange whimpering. Although he was certain that the sound was being made by an Indian, it was unfamiliar to him.

139

His eyes darted between the line of tepees to one side of him and the skittish ponies to the other. He then concentrated on the gentle but eerie noise that continued to come from the dark foliage before him.

'Who's there?' Iron Eyes whispered in the language of the Indians. 'Speak up or I will kill you.'

As he cautiously stepped toward the noise, it grew louder.

Iron Eyes held the knife tighter. The ponies shied away from the tall stranger and gathered at the far end of the roped off enclosure.

'Speak or die,' he threatened in a low growl.

Yet whatever it was that was drawing his attention continued to ignore his pleas. Iron Eyes could not understand what was happening, but realized that it could not be an Indian warrior or he would have been cut down by one of their arrows.

His heightened nerves had only just started to calm down when suddenly he saw something move in the depths of darkness directly before him. His keen vision could just make out that it was the shape of someone moving.

'There you are,' Iron Eyes gritted his teeth and lowered his head until his mane of hair covered his determined features. He started to snort like an outraged buffalo.

The savage nature of the wild beast swelled up inside his chest as he defied his fears and continued on toward whatever was making the strange noises.

Staring through the limp strands of hair hung that

hung lifelessly over his face, Iron Eyes raised his knife level with his chest and then gritted his teeth.

Iron Eyes charged into the shadows.

NINETEEN

Driven by a mixture of trepidation and outright fear, Iron Eyes charged into the shadowy corner of the pony enclosure wielding his knife. The gaunt figure knew that whoever it was lurking in the depths of the blackness, he had to either knock them senseless or silence them permanently before they alerted the rest of the tribe.

As Iron Eyes hurtled into the shadows he had every intention of killing whatever was hidden within it. Then as he was barely five feet from his target his unblinking eyes saw what he was charging at.

It was a sight that totally shocked him.

Somehow he managed to stop his long-legged body before he crashed into the small female. The blade of his lethal dagger was only inches from her buckskin-clad torso as Iron Eyes came to a halt beside her.

Even though no light could penetrate the shadows, their eyes focused on one another. He eased his long frame back a few inches and studied her as she continued to whimper.

The Indian girl had a crude gag in her mouth. She wore a short fringed dress made from rawhide and her exposed legs and arms were cut and bruised. Iron Eyes noticed she was bound to a wooden stake. Both her hands and feet had strips of rawhide tied so tightly that they were cutting into her flesh.

His bony fingers pulled the gag from her mouth and cast it into the mud. She looked up at him with large grateful eyes as he stood beside her in stunned amazement.

'Help me,' she whispered as tears rolled down her face.

Iron Eyes suddenly realized that he understood her. Years of eavesdropping had made it far easier than communicating with the white men at Silver Creek.

'Please help me,' she repeated.

Without uttering a word, Iron Eyes slid the honed edge of his knife blade under each strip of rawhide and cut the leathers. As he sliced the restraints that were holding her arms above her head, she slumped to the ground.

He knelt beside her and touched her cheek.

'Why your people do this to you?' he asked as he gently helped her back to her feet.

She lowered her eyes as if ashamed. 'They say I have been a bad squaw. They punish me.'

Anger swelled up inside the tall young hunter as

he glanced between the nearby tepees at the majority of the tribe. He then looked back at her.

'What did you do?' he naïvely asked.

She looked embarrassed and glanced away from the tall man beside her shapely form.

'It is what I would not do which angered them,' she sighed. 'They punish me because I would not become Chief's new wife.'

Iron Eyes frowned as he stared at the tiny young female in bewilderment. He had never been so close to anyone of her gender before and it confused him. Her scent was like nothing he had ever sensed before and she looked delicate. He touched her braided hair.

'What is a wife?' he muttered. 'I do not savvy your words.'

Her beautiful eyes fluttered as they looked at him. Her hands then rose to her mouth as though attempting to subdue her sudden realization.

'You must be Ayan-Ees,' she gasped through her fingers.

His expression altered. 'You know who I am?'

She nodded but kept her eyes averted from his curious face. 'I know who you are. You are the one they call the evil one. My people hate you.'

Iron Eyes grinned. 'I hate them.'

She moved out of the dense shadows and looked at the cuts on her wrists before glancing up at him. There was urgency in her handsome expression.

'We must flee,' she said. 'They will kill both of us.'

144

'Why would they kill you?' Iron Eyes wondered. 'You are Injun like them. I do not understand.'

She gripped his arm and looked up into his face. 'I was being punished and you cut me free, Ayan-Ees. For that they will kill the both of us.'

Iron Eyes was no wiser as he pulled away from her and then paced toward the skittish ponies. He vainly tried to corner one of them but they kept their distance. After a few endless attempts, he stopped and rested his knuckles on his hips.

'This is not going to be as easy as I thought,' he growled. 'Ponies scared of me.'

The young female hobbled to his side.

'You are going to steal a pony?' she asked in surprise. 'Is that why you are here? You come to steal a pony?'

Iron Eyes glanced briefly at her and then returned his attention to the small muscular mounts.

'This is why I am here,' he nodded.

'I thought you had come to save me,' she shyly sighed.

Iron Eyes did not comprehend her words. He raised an eyebrow but said nothing as he tried to work out how he was going to achieve his ultimate goal.

'You take me away from here?' The female's words almost sounded like begging. She tugged on his shirt sleeve. 'Take me with you.'

'Why?' he asked drily before sliding his knife into his boot neck and rubbing his hands together. 'Why would you want to be with me?'

She moved between Iron Eyes and the ponies to get his attention. Although Iron Eyes was at least a foot taller than the petite female and could still see the ponies quite clearly over her head, he lowered his eyes and looked at her.

'My people will kill us both,' she repeated her warning.

Iron Eyes studied her carefully. She had been brutally whipped, judging by the scars on her naked arms and legs, he thought. Then he noticed that she was bleeding from the wounds on her wrists and ankles. The fringed buckskin dress was tattered and torn and barely covered her well-proportioned body. A desire swelled up inside the naïve young hunter which he neither understood nor cared for. Long-supressed feelings were awaking in Iron Eyes, and this troubled him.

'Can you climb trees?' he asked as he began to doubt that he was ever going to corner any of the ponies. 'I think the only way to escape is by climbing the trees.'

She looked over her shoulder at the ponies and then back at the frustrated hunter. She placed a small hand on his chest and drew his full attention.

'You want ponies?' she asked.

'I did,' he snorted in reluctant admission that for once he had failed to achieve his goal. 'I cannot even catch one let alone ride it out of here.'

She moved even closer to the tall youngster. His

flared nostrils filled with her natural perfume.

'I can get us ponies,' she smiled. 'I can ride like a warrior. You want ponies?'

Iron Eyes gave a firm nod of his head. 'Yes, I want ponies. You can catch them?'

To his utter surprise he watched as the young female moved toward the group of small horses. They did not shy or run away from the tiny female as she approached them. Iron Eyes was stunned when he saw her grab their manes and fearlessly lead two of them back to where he stood.

'Here,' she beamed. 'We must go now. Fast.'

Iron Eyes bit his lower lip and cautiously walked around the strange creatures as they flicked their tails. The ponies looked a lot bigger up close.

He looked over the back of the closest pony at the female.

'What's your name?' he asked.

'My name is Ketna-Toi,' she willingly informed her saviour.

'Fire Bird,' Iron Eyes translated her name without even noticing that he had done so. 'Good name.'

Fire Bird held the mane of her pony and then threw her tiny form up on to the animal's back. She straddled the pony and then encouraged her tall companion to do the same.

It was only because of Iron Eyes' long legs that he managed the feat and found himself sitting astride the grey pony. Again he was disillusioned by the way it felt to actually sit astride a pony.

'This hurts,' he grumbled as the unfamiliar sensation of having his legs so far apart chafed his manhood. 'I do not like this at all, Fire Bird.'

She could not hide her amusement at his discomfort. Then her senses were alerted to the rest of her tribe. She glanced over her shoulder as she heard the sound of warriors heading toward them.

'We must go now,' Fire Bird urged.

'Wait,' Iron Eyes said as he dug out his box of matches and carefully scratched one. The flame lit up his gaunt features as he carefully guided the pony toward one of the tepees. He leaned across to the tent and carefully placed the match under a huge bear skin draped across its side. Flames raced like a speeding locomotive across the tinder-dry fur and then engulfed the tepee. 'Now we go.'

Fire Bird gripped the pony between her thighs and leaned forward. She then kicked and got the sturdy animal moving at the gap in the bushes which Iron Eyes had used to enter the enclosure.

'Follow me, Ayan-Ees,' she called out to her inexperienced companion as he steered his mount away from the roaring inferno he had just created.

Iron Eyes held on to the mane of his mount and copied the actions of the feisty female.

Both ponies tore through the choking smoke and ploughed through the surrounding undergrowth. They raced passed the tepees and turned into the trees. As the ponies gathered momentum, both Fire Bird and Iron Eyes could hear the raised voices of the hysterical Indians behind them.

As they rode into the ever-darkening depths of the woodland they heard another sound. The unmistakable noise only arrows make when flying from bowstrings. Both riders ducked close to the necks of their mounts as a swarm of arrows peppered the trees all around them.

'Where are we going, Ayan-Ees?' she shouted back at the novice horseman behind the tail of her spirited pony.

'We go to my camp,' he shouted back at the buckskin-clad female. 'We gotta get my whiskey and cigars.'

The petite young woman did not understand what either of the items were. She looked back. Iron Eyes grimly rode through shafts of moonlight after her. She allowed her pony to slow down so that he could draw level with her.

'What are whiskey and cigars, Ayan-Ees?' she asked the uncomfortable horseman. 'I do not understand.'

His screwed up face looked at her as his mind raced in searched for a suitable translation.

'Have you heard of firewater and peace pipes?' he yelled.

She nodded and then considered her companion. Everything she had ever heard about the legendary Ayan-Ees from her fellow Indians made no sense. He certainly did not look evil to her as he clung on to the pony beneath him. Iron Eyes just looked in pain as he bounced up and down on the back of the muscular mount. Her pony picked up pace and raced ahead of his.

Fire Bird looked back at Iron Eyes as he desperately clung on to the pony. 'Then what is your plan?'

Iron Eyes had no plan. He was baffled that he had managed to steal one of the Indians' ponies as well as one of their women without getting killed.

'I'm working on it,' he lied.

It seemed as though they had been riding for hours to Iron Eyes as he gripped the mane of his galloping pony beneath him and followed the tail of Fire Bird's pony through the dense moonlit trees. Yet it had only taken minutes to travel the few miles from the Indian encampment. As they rode up a muddy rise both of the riders noticed a wall of flickering flames ahead of them.

Fire Bird pulled back on the mane of her mount and stopped the snorting animal in its tracks as Iron Eyes duplicated her actions. His mount came to a shuddering stop beside the confident female. Both ponies dropped their heads and started to eat as Iron Eyes and Fire Bird stared through the trees at the strange illumination. Nearly a hundred fiery torches made an ominous sight when viewed through the dense undergrowth.

'What is that, Ayan-Ees?' she fearfully asked her haunting companion as he winced in pain atop the pony. He glanced up through his long lank hair at the sight before them.

'I'm not sure,' he replied as his bullet-coloured

eyes narrowed and focused on the flames ahead of them. 'Whatever it is, it's coming this way.'

'We should turn back,' Fire Bird said hastily.

Iron Eyes looked over his wide shoulder and gritted his teeth as he caught sight of a dozen or more Indians riding after them. He shook his head and spat at the ground as the true enormity of the situation dawned on him.

'I can see ten or twelve Injuns riding after us, Fire Bird,' he sighed. 'I reckon they want their horses back.'

She lowered her head.

'We are trapped,' she said. For the first time since he had met the female he detected defeat in her voice. 'Death rides at us from both sides.'

Iron Eyes reached out and patted her shoulder reassuringly. Her tearful eyes looked at him.

'We are still alive, Fire Bird,' he said firmly. 'Death has not claimed us yet. We have time.'

Fire Bird straightened up and looked at Iron Eyes as he continued to watch the eerie light. She moved her pony closer to him.

'Is the forest on fire?' she stammered.

He shook his head and pushed his limp hair off his face as he continued to watch the moving lights. He sniffed at the air and then gritted his teeth.

'That is the smell of white men,' he stated. 'They burn oil in their town to make light. This smells the same.'

'White men?' Fire Bird sounded frightened as she

151

repeated his words. 'The same white men that cut down the trees and forced my tribe to move from our ancestral home?'

Iron Eyes nodded. 'I reckon so, Fire Bird.'

The young Indian girl looked terrified as she glanced back and listened to the riders getting closer with each beat of her pounding young heart. Fire Bird returned her attention to the fiery torches.

'What do the white men want?' she asked.

'Me by the looks of it,' he surmised. 'They want me.'

'But why do the white men want you, Ayan-Ees?' she could not hide her fear from the man who had saved her life. 'Have you stolen their ponies?'

Iron Eyes shook his head. 'No.'

'Then why do they want you?' she pressed.

He rubbed his jaw and shrugged. The words of warning which the blacksmith had uttered after he had killed Drew Smith flooded back into the young hunter's mind.

'They just want to kill me, Fire Bird,' Iron Eyes sighed heavily. 'It's what the white men call vengeance.'

'I don't know this word?' Fire Bird said fearfully. 'What does it mean?'

He shook his head. 'I'm not sure.'

Iron Eyes cast his attention at the flaming torches and then looked back at the Indians. The hunter could see their screaming faces daubed in paint as they charged through the scattering of moonlight shafts.

He bit his lip and then pulled the bow off his shoulder and drew an arrow from its leather quiver. His long fingers carefully placed the arrow on the bowstring.

'I reckon it means that I've got even more enemies than I figured, Fire Bird,' he said before turning on the pony and facing the galloping Indians. He drew the string back and then fired. He then swiftly threw his long right leg over the neck of his pony and as he slid to the ground he looked up at the trusting female and smiled.

'Ride, Fire Bird,' he whispered. 'Take the ponies and ride like the wind. You are not safe with either the lumberjacks or your people. Ride.'

Fire Bird was going to argue and then realized that it would be pointless. Her left hand took hold of his mount's mane, turned both animals and then kicked her bare feet back.

Iron Eyes fired another arrow and then heard the deathly response. The advancing Indians had released their own arrows at him. The forest buzzed as the lethal projectiles flew through the eerie light at the gaunt hunter.

His pitifully thin frame had only just managed to duck behind a tree when arrows hammered into its trunk or passed between the slender elms and on toward the advancing lumberjacks.

Iron Eyes looked and saw Fire Bird riding deep into the undergrowth before he pulled another arrow from his quiver and charged the bow once more.

Suddenly more arrows cut passed him.

He squinted hard at the fiery torches and heard the cries of lumberjacks as some of the arrows hit them. He swallowed hard and then tossed the bow aside as his skeletal hand drew one of the guns from his belt. He cocked and fired the six-shooter at the Indians and then athletically climbed up the tree into its overhanging branches.

No sooner had Iron Eyes come to rest on a sturdy leaf draped branch when the Indian riders thundered between the trees below him. Just like the lumberjacks, they wanted to find and kill the elusive Iron Eyes. Their whooping and feverish cries echoed around the forest. The Indians did not stop their war cries until they rode straight into the lumberjacks' ranks.

Suddenly, as Iron Eyes crouched on the branch, he witnessed the darkness light up as the loggers' guns exploded into action. The deafening noise was chilling, even to the young observer as he watched the bloody battle.

The gut-wrenching screams filled the forest as both sides fought for their very lives. Neither side showed the other any mercy. Ponies raced back toward the Indian encampment. Iron Eyes stared down through the shadows and noticed that every single one of the ponies was drenched in the blood of its master.

A handful of heartbeats later, the forest had fallen strangely silent. The brief but gory battle was over.

Iron Eyes clambered back down to the ground and stood like a statue staring into the gunsmoke-filled air.

He cautiously moved with the six-gun still in his hand toward the site of the brutal encounter. The sight of carnage stunned the tall youth as he finally reached the place where both the lumberjacks and the Indians had unwittingly crashed into each other.

Iron Eyes gazed at the bodies that littered the woodland floor and shook his head silently. Even the fleeting moonlight could not disguise the blood-covered ground. A couple of maimed ponies had suffered the same fate as their riders and had been either shot or stabbed in the heat of battle. Bodies were strewn everywhere and every one of them was dead.

His narrowed eyes looked up and noted the feverish retreat of the majority of the lumberjacks as they fled with their fiery torches back toward Silver Creek.

He could see the lumberjacks assisting the wounded through the long grass. Iron Eyes studied the bodies at his feet and then noticed the familiar features of Hog Barker staring with dead eyes up at the tree canopies.

The long-legged hunter nodded to himself at the sight of the arrow-filled man who had caused him so much unwanted attention earlier that day. A satisfied smirk etched his haunting face before he turned on his heels and raced through the dense undergrowth back toward the den where he had earlier left his goods. He dragged the box out into the murky moonlight and quickly tore a cork from a whiskey bottle and downed a third of its contents. The fumes of the hard liquor filled his exhausted mind as its contents burned its way down into his craw.

As he placed one of the cigars from the box between his teeth he heard the sound of unshod hoofs behind his broad back. Iron Eyes turned and stared through the drifting cloud of gunsmoke as the young Indian girl rode through its ghostly mist toward him leading his pony beside her own.

Fire Bird dismounted and ran up to him. Her arms wrapped around his middle and squeezed his lean frame tightly.

'You are safe, Ayan-Ees,' she sobbed thankfully. 'I heard the fight and thought you must be dead.'

Iron Eyes pulled out a match and ignited it with his thumbnail and touched the end of the cigar with its flickering flame. He inhaled the smoke deeply and then exhaled above her head. As she looked up at him, he nodded.

'I do not die that easy, Fire Bird,' he said stroking her braided hair. 'They tried to kill me and ended up killing each other.'

Fire Bird watched as he pulled away from her and raised the bottle to his lips again. As the burning whiskey made its way down his throat, he returned the cigar to his mouth and inhaled deeply.

'Soon the rest of my tribe's warriors will come to this part of the forest,' Fire Bird said as she stared at the crimson-stained ground. 'They will be looking for my body and yours and when they do not find them, they will hunt us down.'

Iron Eyes nodded.

'You are right, we must leave this place,' he said through a cloud of cigar smoke. 'I cannot leave you here to suffer the wrath of your people alone. I must take you with me.'

She moved closer to her tall companion. 'Will we be safe out there in the land of the white men, Ayan-Ees?'

'Maybe,' Iron Eyes shrugged and somehow managed to mount the pony as Fire Bird threw herself on to the back of her own horse. She stared at her strange companion as he chewed thoughtfully on his cigar.

'We go now?' she asked.

'We go now,' Iron Eyes agreed.

The two ponies headed out of the forested terrain and slowly moved through the moonlight away from Silver Creek.

FINALE

The unmistakable sound of the stagecoach drew the attention of the heavily-scarred Iron Eyes. He turned on his ornate saddle and sucked the last of his cigar's smoke before tossing it aside. He turned the high-shouldered palomino stallion and watched as Squirrel Sally drove her six-horse team across the rolling range toward him.

The morning sun made the fiery female's mane of long hair look as though it were spun from precious gold.

Smoke filtered through his teeth as the stagecoach drew to a halt before the powerful stallion. Sally rested her bare foot on the brake pole and stared down at the man who she refused to ever let get too far away from her.

'What in tarnation are you doing, you ugly galoot?' she asked before poking her pipe between her teeth and scratching a match across the driving board. She puffed a few times and then looked down upon the thoughtful horseman.

'I was just thinking,' Iron Eyes replied as he turned the horse full circle to study the terrain.

'What was you thinking about, my beloved?' Sally asked before tossing the spent match over her shoulder on to the stagecoach roof.

He sighed. 'I was just recalling a few things, Squirrel.'

'And what was you recalling?' she grinned.

'I was recalling a time long ago when I met a real pretty little Injun gal, Squirrel,' he replied before turning his palomino away from the stagecoach and tapping his spurs.

Sally's eyebrows rose up into her fringe.

'And who exactly was this real pretty Injun gal, Iron Eyes?' she snorted angrily at him as he slowly rode away from the feisty female. 'Well? Who is she? Where is she?'

Iron Eyes looked over his wide shoulder.

'That's another story, Squirrel,' he answered.